MW00642128

Promise Me, Cowboy

Promise Me, Cowboy

A Copper Mountain Rodeo novella

CJ Carmichael

Promise Me, Cowboy

Copyright© 2013 CJ Carmichael

Tule Publishing First Printing, August 2017

The Tule Publishing Group, LLC

ALL RIGHTS RESERVED

No part of this book may be used or reproduced in any manner whatsoever without written permission except in the case of brief quotations embodied in critical articles and reviews.

This is a work of fiction. Names, characters, places, and incidents are products of the author's imagination or are used fictitiously. Any resemblance to actual events, locales, organizations, or persons, living or dead, is entirely coincidental.

ISBN: 978-1-947636-17-0

Dedication

For Jane, Melissa and Megan. I'll never forget our wonderful Montana adventure, or how much stuff you were able to pack into the trunk of my car.

Dear Reader,

Is it possible for one weekend to change your life?

Yes. And that's exactly what happens when the Copper Mountain Rodeo comes to Marietta, Montana this year.

In my story Sage Carrigan, local chocolatier, is going to have to decide whether she can forgive cowboy Dawson O'Dell for a terrible mistake he made five years ago.

I had a lot of fun packing this story with some of my very favorite things. Like gorgeous mountain scenery. Characters to root for, and characters to drive you crazy. And chocolate! Sage, who owns Copper Mountain Chocolate, creates all her products from scratch. I'd always wondered how to make chocolate and what my research told me was—it isn't easy. Thank goodness there are so many wonderful chocolatiers who are willing to do all that hard work for us!

What else is in the book? Well, it's a reunion story, which is one of my favorite types of romances... especially when they involve a cowboy with a wild past who is willing to change his ways for the right woman.

Chapter One awaits... I hope you enjoy. And please come back for more stories about the Carrigans Of The Circle C. I'm working on them right now!

Happy Reading,
CJ

Chapter One

A LOT OF people believe you can't keep a secret in a small town, but that simply wasn't true. Sage Carrigan was only twenty-nine years old and already she had two that would blow the minds of her sisters and her father and the girlfriends who thought they knew every little thing about her.

And one of those secrets was just now stepping into her chocolate shop.

Sage stepped behind the counter, needing something solid to lean on. It was really him, Dawson O'Dell, her biggest secret, her biggest mistake… her biggest weakness.

Right now O'Dell was one of the top ranked cowboys in professional rodeo. She'd met him back in her barrel-racing days, but five years hadn't changed him much. He still dressed like the bronc-rider he was, in Wrangler jeans and dusty boots, western shirt unbuttoned to the white T shirt beneath. His dark blonde hair was a little too long, and his green eyes a little too astute.

The second his eyes met hers she knew this was no

chance encounter.

"Sage."

He walked right up to the counter and gave her a look that made her instantly remember all the things she had once found so irresistible about this man.

"It's been a long time," he added.

He looked at her as if he knew her inside and out. Which he did. Or at least *he had.* Then his gaze swept the shop, the shelves of attractively packaged chocolate. However you liked it, she had it. Dark chocolate covering silky mint creams, milk chocolate over salt-flecked toffee, chocolate shavings and chocolate mixed with nuts. Bars of dark, milk or white chocolate. Chocolate in the shape of horses, cowboy boots…or the letters from A to Z. And more.

"Quite a departure from barrel-racing."

"That was kind of the point." Finally she'd found her voice. And now that the shock of seeing him was settling down, anger began seeping into its place. "If you're here to buy something—please do it quickly. Otherwise, it would be best if you just left." She looked pointedly at the door, hoping she'd kept the nerves out of her voice.

He rubbed the side of his face, using his left hand. No wedding ring, she noticed. But then there hadn't been last time, either.

He gave her a lopsided smile. "Sounds like you're still a little angry."

"I'm not angry, O'Dell. Just really not interested in seeing you. Or talking to you. Or even breathing the same air as you."

His eyebrows went up. "That's harsh."

Obviously not harsh enough because he didn't leave. Instead he wandered to the display of chocolate letters and selected an "S."

For Sage?

"I owe you an apology," he allowed.

"Five years ago you owed me an apology. Now, you just need to walk out that door and let me go on pretending I never met you."

He sighed like she was the dolt in the classroom who just didn't *get it.* "I did *try* to apologize. But you left town mighty fast."

Less than twenty-four hours after she crashed on that second barrel, her father had shown up in Casper, Wyoming and had whisked her home. But there *had* been time for Dawson to reach her. If he'd wanted to.

That had been the last rodeo she'd ever competed in. And it had been the last time she'd let herself get tangled up with a cowboy, too.

"Sage, even if it is a little late, I still want to say it. I was sorry then, and I'm sorry now."

Damn, if he didn't look sincere. But she hardened her heart. Facts were facts and how sorry could he be if he'd waited so long to find her?

Keeping her tone artificially sweet, she asked, "What exactly are you sorry for? Would that be for sleeping with me even though you were married?"

He winced.

"Or for your wife catching me butt naked in your bed and then pointing a rifle in my face?"

His gaze dropped to the counter and he swallowed hard. The words—she'd never spoken them aloud before—hung out there, embarrassing, and true, damn it. All too true.

"Sure sounds bad, when you put it like that."

"They are the plain and simple facts Now, may I point you in the direction of the door one more time?" She glanced out the window, seeing scores of shoppers out on the street. *Would one of you please come in and buy some chocolate? Save me from having to say anything more to this guy?*

"I'll be on my way soon," he promised. "Let me pay for this first." He put the "S" on the counter. He'd chosen milk chocolate. She preferred dark.

"That'll be ten dollars."

His eyebrows went up. "That's a lot of money for one piece of chocolate."

"It's premium quality. Made from scratch in-house. I buy the beans myself, directly from Venezuela. But if you want to put it back, go right ahead."

"No, no, I'll take it." He pulled out his wallet and counted out a five and some ones.

"For someone special?" she couldn't resist asking, after placing the confection in a cute paper bag and tying the handles with some copper ribbon. “Susan, maybe? Sandra? Sonya?”

“Savannah, actually.”

She was such a fool for thinking, for even a second, that he’d selected it for her. “Here you go.”

As she handed him the bag, she noticed him checking out her fingers. Oh my God, was he looking to see if she was married, too? What about this Savannah girl? The man was incorrigible.

And lucky. She couldn’t believe they hadn’t been interrupted by another customer during all this time.

“O’Dell?” He was looking at her like she was a toy in a catalogue that he couldn’t afford. “Shouldn’t you be leaving now?”

“Yup. Just wanted to say, it was nice to see you, Sage. You’re even prettier than I remembered.”

She couldn’t help softening at those words, and the sincere look in his eyes as he said them. But then she remembered how she’d felt staring down the barrel of that shotgun, and her resolve was back, stronger than ever. “Goodbye, O’Dell.”

On his way out the door, he turned over the “Open” sign in the window.

Had he… ?

He gave her a wink and another one of his killer smiles. “Didn’t want anyone walking in on us, did I?”

Damn it, he had.

But she still managed to get the last word. "You mean like last time?"

DAWSON DROPPED THE smile, along with the pretense of being cool and collected, the moment he left Sage's store. That had been harder than he'd thought it would be. But he hadn't lied when he said it was good to see her, because it had been. Damn good.

He knew he deserved every bit of her cool disdain.

But he'd hoped to see a crack in the veneer. There'd been one sweet second when he'd caught a glimpse of something that wasn't hatred in her eyes. But then it was gone and all that was left was a solid concrete wall, with her on one side and him on the other.

Well. He'd said his apology at least. Taken the first step.

He took a moment to soak in the ambiance of Marietta, Montana. It was cool in the shade, but if you stepped into the sun you could almost believe you'd been transported back to summer. He liked the look of the park in front of the Courthouse. And the way Copper Mountain shone above the town, sunlight glinting off the granite facets.

It was a real town, solid and also beautiful.

He just hoped he hadn't made a big mistake coming here.

DAWSON WAS IN town for the rodeo, Sage supposed. But had it really been necessary for him to come to *her* town? There were rodeos all over this country and he had to pick Copper Mountain Rodeo in Marietta Montana. Volunteers and shop owners had been getting ready for weeks. There were banners on Main Street and most of the stores had a western-themed display in their front window. Last night she had coerced her friend Jenny into helping her set out bales of hay, and a rusted wagon wheel in her own window, using them as background for her display of pretty copper boxes.

Poor Jenny. Her big fancy wedding had been called off and she was really beside herself. But maybe it had been for the best. Sage hadn't been all that fond of Charles.

Hopefully the rodeo would distract Jenny from her heartache. The kick-off was happening tomorrow night with street dancing and a fund-raising dinner. In the morning the barricades would go up, blocking off traffic from the three blocks that were considered the heart of the town.

Sage's shop was within this area and she was expecting her chocolate cowboy boots to sell like crazy. Not so much the hot chocolate—that was a big hit in winter. But she'd just started making chocolate dipped frozen vanilla yogurt bars and she suspected she'd have a run on those as well.

With the store sign saying "Open" once more, customers resumed coming in, some to browse, but most to buy. She noticed her hands trembling as she counted out change to the first few of them.

Damn that O'Dell. After all this time he should have just *let it be.*

AT SIX O'CLOCK Sage closed her shop, dropped a deposit off at the bank, then got on her bike to cycle home. As usual her route took her along Bramble Lane, the nicest street in town, with stately brick and stone homes on one side and the Marietta River on the other. Many of the original mining magnates who had built this town on the profits of copper, had chosen this road for home.

Her own mother, Beverly Bramble, had descended from one of those families, and not only this street, but also the family home, still bore their name. Sage was passing it now, a red brick mansion on a stone foundation with white trim and a gracious porch. There was a turret above the porch and a widow's walk to the left of that.

When her mother was still alive, she used to take Sage and her three sisters to have tea with great-aunt Mabel once a month. That tradition had died, along with her mother, over fifteen-years ago. But great-aunt Mabel still lived on—now supported by a grand-niece who had turned most of the bedrooms in the old mansion into guest rooms.

Sage still popped in on the old lady now and then. But Mabel was so rude, she never looked forward to those visits and suspected her great-aunt didn't get much enjoyment out of them either.

She only continued them as a nod to her mother's memory.

Several blocks further on Bramble Lane, past the mansions, were some more modest homes. Sage hit her brakes when she saw a 'Conditional Sale' sign on a pretty two-story with a red door and a charming stone walkway. The house had been for sale for almost three months. Now it seemed, someone had made a serious offer.

She stuck out her bottom lip, disappointed. Not that she had the money for a down payment—she's checked the price and it was too high. But while the house was on the market, at least she'd been able to *dream.*

Sage placed her foot back on the pedal of her bike, then pushed off, continuing down Bramble Lane then taking a left toward the center of town. She loved cycling to and from work, but never more than in the autumn when the cottonwoods were golden and the air was as crisp as the Spartan apples that grew in the valleys up north of Marietta.

At the next street she began to feel the old ache in her knee like a whisper from her past. Not so much pain as a reminder of what happened when you tried to please someone else, rather than yourself.

The days of trying to impress her dad were over for her now. It had been an uphill battle from the start, since she'd been born a girl, rather than a boy, the third of four sisters, the quiet one of the bunch, pretty but not beautiful like Mattie, reasonably intelligent but not brilliant like Dani, and, God knows, nowhere near as tough and brave as Callan who still lived and worked on the family ranch with their dad.

When she reached the house she was currently renting—small and utterly charmless compared to the Bramble Lane one—Sage wheeled her bike into the garage, then headed in the back door to the kitchen where she exchanged her bike helmet and gloves for her purse and a box of the salted caramels from the fridge holding her extra inventory. She thought about changing her outfit. It was family reunion time at the Circle C Ranch tonight. Though Dani lived in Seattle, and Mattie and Wes had a spread up near Missoula, they always came home for the Copper Mountain Rodeo. The night before festivities officially began was family night, marked by a big barbecue at the ranch house.

Sage opened her closet door to consider her choices. But the sight of the pumpkin-colored taffeta she'd worn for Jenny's aborted wedding was so depressing she decided she would go as she was.

One day soon she needed to put that dress in a box… or maybe sell it to a consignment clothing shop.

The drive to the Circle C was a long and beautiful one, winding along the valley that cut through the Gallatin Range to her right and the Absarokas to her left. Here there were miles and miles between neighbors. Most of the land was owned by just three families.

First were the MacCreadies, whose ranch house and outbuildings were about half-an-hour from Marietta. Mrs. MacCreadie was the sweetest woman, but she'd gone a little strange after the birth of her triplets—which had come just a year after her second child.

"You'd have to lock me away in a mental institution if that happened to me," Sage remembered her mother saying. Now *her* parents had known how to use birth control. At least four years were between her and each of her sisters.

Tucked deeper into the valley, she knew, was the Douglases place. But tragedy had made that ranch a place she preferred not to think about. One of her sisters—she was pretty sure it had been Mattie—used to babysit for the Douglases. Before.

One of her favorite Lady Antebellum songs started to play and she turned up the volume on the radio.

Fifteen minutes farther she came to the Sheenan's spread. Bill and his wife had had a boy to match every one of the Carrigan girls, but they'd had very little to do with one another in school. Water rights were what it was all about when you were a rancher and Bill and her father had an ongoing feud about the mountain-fed stream that ran along the border of their properties. They both had the right to use that water, but over the years both Bill and her own father had been guilty of some surreptitious damming and diverting.

Sage didn't know who had started it.

And she didn't care.

She had something else against the Sheenans… *Secret number two.*

HER DAD WAS barbecuing hearty beef ribs on the back deck when she arrived. Hawksley Carrigan wasn't the sort of father who took to hugging and kissing, so she patted his shoulder as she walked by. His hair was the usual gray tangle, but his face seemed to age every time she saw him lately. More deep grooves in the sun-baked skin. Fallen jowls and bushy eyebrows that made him seem even more forbidding than he had when he was younger.

"'bout time you got here."

"The shop closes at six, Dad." Of course, mentioning that was like barbecuing salmon during wasp season—looking to get stung. Her father could not understand why she'd gone into business making and selling hand-made chocolates. If Hawksley had his way, she'd still be living on the ranch and barrel-racing—despite her injured knee.

"Where's Wes?" Mattie's husband was usually out on the deck with her father. Not that the two men liked each other much. But when it came to barbecuing meat—the men knew where they belonged.

"Didn't come this time."

That was a first. Knowing better than to try and coax the reason for this from her father, she headed for the kitchen, the biggest room in the house, but also, paradoxically, the coziest.

Mattie was at the butcher block island, chopping veggies for a salad. Callan was pulling the nice dishes out from the glass-fronted, built-in maple cabinetry. As for Dani—well, the brains of the family was drinking wine and supervising.

"Hey, sisters! I'm here!" She slipped her box of chocolates on the counter by the phone where they wouldn't get in the way, then targeted her oldest sister with a kiss. "Mattie—where's Wes?"

Mattie was petite and slim-waisted, with curves that seemed almost indecent on such a little woman. She had the same dark hair as all the Carrigans—all but Sage, who'd pulled the recessive red hair gene wild card.

Though Mattie was only thirty-eight, Sage could see signs of aging that hadn't been present during their last visit. Fine lines bracketing Mattie's lovely smile and a tired look in her milk chocolate eyes.

"Oh, Wes decided to compete in a rodeo down in Utah this weekend."

That didn't make sense. For as long as Wes and Mattie had been together, Wes had signed up for the Copper Mountain Rodeo. Usually they brought their twins with them. But the girls had left this fall for their first year of University.

After a warning look from Callan, who was also tiny like Mattie, only with a more boyish figure, Sage decided not to question her older sister any further. Instead she gave Dani a hug. "How is life in the ivory tower in Seattle?"

Dani, who'd recently been promoted to full professor in the psychology department of the University of Washington, dragged her gaze up from her Blackberry. "Very busy. Very exciting." The second eldest sister, Dani was taller, like Sage. Not as fine-boned as the others. More average. Though she definitely carried more weight than Sage.

Office work, Sage supposed. Professional dinners and travel. That sort of thing.

"How do you stay so slim?" Dani's mind was on the same subject. Her gaze ran over Sage in her cropped pants and peach-colored top. "You make chocolates for a living. You should be roly-poly by now."

"I *make* them. Then *sell* them. I would think a smart woman like you would understand the concept of *profit.*"

"You never sample?"

"Oh, I have minions for that."

Everyone laughed, because if there was one thing Sage didn't have, it was minions. Two part-time employees who helped cover sales during busy times and on weekends, that was it.

God this is good. Sage savored the moment, because it didn't happen often that the four of them loosened up this way. Their father had raised them to keep their heads up. At any moment you could be chastised for doing the wrong thing or for not doing the right thing. Dani and Mattie had resented him bitterly. Only Callan seemed to be able to shrug off his barbs, often giving as good as she got.

As for Sage, she thought she understood what was behind her father's bitterness and anger, and so she made allowances. But then she knew things that her sisters didn't.

"—and I told him I *so* wasn't going out with him again. Then I left the restaurant and caught a ride home with a friend." This was Callan, talking about her latest romantic escapade, Sage supposed. She'd tuned out for a bit. Callan always had fun stories to tell, whether they were about her love life—very active—or about ranching trials and tribulations. There were lots of those, too.

"Sometimes I wish I hadn't married so young." Mattie, normally so pragmatic and solid, sounded atypically yearning. "I never had a chance to date and have fun like you, Cal."

"*Nobody* has dated as much as Callan," Dani said. "That includes me and I'm still single and eight years older!"

They all looked at Sage then. Dani, never one for the subtle approach, was the first to ask. "So, how are things with Toby?"

"Over." Callan answered for her.

"But—why? Was it the age difference? He was in your class at school, wasn't he Mat?"

"Yes. And he's a good guy. But just let Sage be. You know she doesn't like talking about stuff like this."

Sage shrugged. She never found it easy discussing anything personal. *And why was that?* She'd assumed it was just her personality.

But suddenly she remembered her mother saying something to her only a few months before she died. They'd been right here, in the kitchen, and Sage had been twelve. Bev Carrigan had leaned over the table and taken Sage's hand in hers. "You used to be such a chatterbox, honey. What's happened to you?"

Sage hadn't said a word, and her mother had sighed. "Guess you're at that age, huh?"

At the time she hadn't realized her mother was talking about adolescence. But those years were long gone and Sage still felt as if there was a fine plastic film separating her from the people she loved. She wished she could just set down the secret and leave it somewhere. But secrets were like land mines. You had to make sure no one stepped on them. Or the whole family might blow apart.

AN HOUR LATER they were gathered around the dining room table, the five of them—just as it had been before Mattie got married and before Dani moved to the city. Some fathers might have deemed the occasion worthy of a toast. Or at least have said something like, "It's good to have all my girls under the same roof again."

Not Hawksley. He did come close to smiling a few times. But when dinner was over, he didn't linger. "Got my show to watch. Sage, you make sure you stay and help clean up.

Don't leave all the work to your sisters."

Dani shook her head disbelievingly after he'd gone. "He never changes. Never."

"I don't mind," Sage said. "He's disappointed I gave up barrel racing."

"Wasn't that five years ago?" Ever the mother, Mattie started stacking the plates.

"Let me do that," Sage said. "Dad's right—I missed all the prep work."

Mattie didn't release her hold. "Because you were *working.* Sage, you have a God-given gift with chocolate. I hope you never let him guilt you into giving up your business."

"I won't," Sage said calmly. Her older sisters were always quick to defend her, and that was sweet. But she wished they would cut their dad a little more slack. "He's looking older, don't you think?"

"He's losing steam on the ranch, too," Callan confided. "He doesn't want to admit it, but he can't work as much as he used to. He said he has to go watch his show—but I'll bet you anything you'll find him sleeping by the TV."

"Maybe we need another hired hand?" Dani asked. They'd cleared off the table and were now in the kitchen, falling back into their old roles easily. Mattie putting away the leftovers, Dani rinsing the plates and handing them to Sage to stack in the dishwasher, while Callan wiped the countertops and appliances.

Again Sage's mother's voice was in her head, as she admired the pattern on the old Royal Albert dishes. "Silly nonsense having nice dishes and never using them. Of course we're going to put them in the dishwasher..."

"I suggested hiring another worker, but he dug in his heels. You know how he can get." Callan shook her head. "I think the only strategy with any hope of success is if I got married. He'd have to let my husband work on the ranch."

"Married? Do you have a candidate in mind?" Mattie had to know.

"You mean just one?"

They all laughed again.

When it came time to leave, Sage felt a little sad. Maybe she should have packed a bag and stayed overnight. She hated to miss any of the fun. But she would see them on Saturday, at the rodeo and then later at the community steak dinner. When she said goodnight, Mattie walked her to her car.

Fallen leaves crunched under their feet as they walked out the side door and the horses by the fence perked up their ears.

"No treats tonight, fellas," Sage told them as she headed for her car.

"You seemed quiet tonight." Mattie put a hand on her shoulder. I mean, you're always quiet. But even more so."

She wasn't surprised Mattie had noticed. Even before the birth of her sister's twins, or the death of their mother, Mattie had had strong maternal instincts. As a child she'd been the one to nurse the orphaned animals, to rescue the bird that had fallen from its nest.

"Yeah, I guess I was." She'd thought about Dawson far too often tonight, despite her determination to forget him. "Is everything okay? With the business?"

She considered telling her sister the whole story. But it was late and she had to work tomorrow. "It's fine. I'm not getting rich. But I'm doing something I love and I'm making a comfortable margin."

Mattie pushed a strand of hair out of her eyes. "Wish I could say the same about our ranch."

Ranching was always a precarious living. That was why Wes, in his late thirties, was still on the rodeo circuit even though he'd injured almost every body part he had. "Is Wes okay?"

"Just between you and me, he's been better. A close buddy of his was killed by a bull when they were at the Crazy Horse Stampede in South Dakota this June. It shook him up pretty badly."

"I guess so." Sage gave her sister a hug. "Is he thinking of quitting the circuit?"

"I don't know. We haven't been talking much. Used to be he'd come home from a rodeo and we'd make love and talk for hours. That hasn't been happening lately."

"I guess all couples go through times like that."

"Sure. We'll get through it." Mattie smiled. "Now you better get going. Drive safe little sister."

Chapter Two

SAGE WOKE EARLY from an unsatisfying sleep. It felt as if she'd been up all night, thinking about Dawson. Or had she been dreaming?

She wished she could dismiss him from her thoughts as easily as she'd shown him the door yesterday. Though, that had actually been difficult, too. There should be a law against a guy breaking a woman's heart, humiliating her, then showing up five years later to remind her why she'd fallen for the jerk in the first place.

Because much as she hated to admit it, she'd felt the old desire the second she'd seen him. It was in the way he carried his cowboy lean-and-tough body. The hint of vulnerability in his disarming grin. And, most of all, the steady light in his green eyes when he looked at her.

No man she'd ever met could compare to him.

And none had ever hurt her nearly as much.

On the bright side—he'd be gone by the end of the rodeo on Sunday. At least she had that to hang onto.

Sage focused on her morning routine, getting dressed

and eating her granola, yogurt and fruit. Her plan was to put in a long day—skipping the street dancing—so she could take tomorrow and Sunday afternoon off and go to the rodeo with her sisters.

But as she rode her bike by the house on Bramble Lane, she found herself thinking of Dawson again. She wished she could call one of her girlfriends—Jenny or Chelsea—to get some advice. *How do I get this guy out of my head?* But that would mean telling them what had happened in the first place.

And she couldn't bring herself to do it.

It had been so damn embarrassing. And infuriating. No matter how attracted she'd been to O'Dell, she never would have gone to his trailer that night if she'd known he was married. She was *so* not that kind of woman. As if to prove the point, she still got hot with embarrassment and shame when she remembered how his wife had walked in on them. They'd been naked, and O'Dell had just pulled himself out of her. Sage thought she might still have been moaning with pleasure.

Then the slamming of the aluminum trailer door. And a woman with big hair and an even bigger voice. "What the hell do you think you're doing with my husband?"

She could just imagine the horrified looks she'd get from her friends. Chelsea and Jenny weren't prudes—but they weren't into casual sex either.

And neither was she, damn it.

The morning sun was casting long shadows over Main Street when she arrived. She pulled into the alley, locking up her bike, then going in via the kitchen. It was a relief to arrive at her shop, because even though she'd been open for three years, it felt like a new thrill every time she stepped inside.

First was the scent—rich cocoa with vanilla, caramel and spice undertones. Mmm—so good. The cocoa and vanilla theme carried through to the decorating in the front show-room. The maple shelves were stained the color of forty-five percent milk chocolate and tiny vases with vanilla colored roses were displayed in a line on the feature wall. In keeping with the name of her store, she used copper-tinted boxes for her chocolates, and these were arranged in attractive displays, delicious little pyramids of hand-made truffles, molded chocolates, and yummy granola bark.

Black and white photos on the wall behind the counter showed every step of the chocolate making process. From buying the beans in Venezuela, roasting and cracking them in her industrial grade kitchen, to conching, refining, tempering and finally molding.

Of course she could have purchased the chocolate in bulk—much easier and cheaper, since she wouldn't have needed to buy any special equipment. But when it came to chocolate Sage was a purist. For her, developing a single-origin bar that defined Copper Mountain Chocolates was her holy grail. The one she'd come up with after a year of experimenting was a seventy-two percent Criollo from Venezuela. Sampling the bar was akin to tasting a fine and rare wine. Initial flavors of cinnamon and hazelnut were followed by notes of caramel and banana, ending with a dry finish.

For most of her products however, her caramels, mints, and the molded chocolate, she used Trinitario beans. Why use premium cocoa beans when the end result was going to be mixed with other flavors?

Sage slipped on a clean apron, she always wore one in the store, then went to look out the front window. Volunteer organizers were already moving barricades into place, and someone was doing sound checks on the stage. She wondered if Dawson would be at the street dance tonight—along with that Savannah woman. Was he cheating again, or had he actually gotten divorced this time?

Sage would never forgot his wife's name, or the way Dawson had looked, scrambling out of bed and pulling on his jeans.

"Calm down, Gina. And would you please stop pointing that gun like that? Give it to me, Gina. Give it to me, damn it."

Not the sort of pillow talk a woman wanted to hear after the best sex of her life.

While Dawson and Gina been tussling over the shotgun, she'd slipped around them, dragging her clothing with her, not stopping to put them on until she was safely behind the next trailer over.

Just her luck a cowboy returning home after a very long night of partying had walked by right then. "Hell," he'd said. "Must have had more to drink than I thought."

"SAGE! OVER HERE!"

Dani was in the bleachers already, along with Mattie, Callan and Dad. They'd nabbed good seats, just above the chutes. Sage waved back and made her way up the aisle, with her beer and corn dog in hand.

She was excited. While the social events were highlights for many of the citizens of Marietta, she loved the rodeo—especially now that she was no longer a competitor. Back in those days, she was often so nervous she vomited before her event. Now it was a luxury to sit back and watch.

"Sorry I'm late." She squeezed into the last seat on the row next to Dani. Unlike the rest of them, Dani's western wear came from expensive boutiques and she looked ready to do a cover shoot for *Montana Woman*. "I was—"

"At your shop," her dad said dryly from the other end of the bench. "Yeah. We know."

Dani rolled her eyes. Then passed her the program. "You missed the opening. Tie-down roping is just about to start."

A quick scan down the names of the contestants—she couldn't help herself—and she found him. Dawson was first on the list.

"This would be so much more interesting if they would include all the cowboys' stats in the program," Dani said. "Then we could calculate their odds at winning."

Sage leaned forward, winking at Callan and Mattie. "You're right, Dani. We should bring that up with the rodeo committee next year."

"Good idea," Callan pretended to agree. "I bet lots of other people would rather look at rows of numbers than a bunch of hot cowboys"

The three sisters laughed, while Dani continued to peer down her nose at the program.

"Would you all be quiet?" Hawksley glowered at them. "I can't hear the announcer."

But Sage could. She heard every word.

"And here we have a boy who's lived just about everywhere, from Reno, Nevada to Denver, Colorado—Mr. Dawson O'Dell. This is Dawson's first time at the Copper Mountain Rodeo. How about we give him a big, down home welcome?"

As the crowd responded, Sage thought she heard a little girl's high voice cheering over the crowd, saying *That's my Daddy!* She turned and scanned the people sitting around her. There were many children on the bleachers but none stood out as the one she'd thought she heard. Anyway, the girl could have been talking about any of the men, from the announcer, to one of the pickup men sitting on the arena fence.

Then the action started and Sage forgot about everything but the cowboy on his horse, racing after the calf. Dawson's rope was in the air and a second later around the animal's neck.

"Damn he's good," she heard Mattie say. "And cute, too."

"Not cute," Callan disputed. "Sexy as hell. Do you know him, Sage?"

"Saw him at a few rodeos back in the day," she admitted, her eyes on the action.

In an astonishing short amount of time—just six point nine seconds—the calf's three legs had been tied and held with a half-hitch knot. The crowd roared in approval, while Dawson clapped the dirt off his hands like it was no big deal. He did pause before leaving the arena though, tipping his hat and smiling at someone in the crowd.

Was he looking at her?

No, someone *behind* her and to her *left.* Just as Sage turned, the little girl called out again, "Way to go, Daddy!"

Sage saw her this time. A cutie about five years old, decked out in a cowboy hat and a T-shirt with a red bandana tied at her throat. Sitting beside her was a tall, striking blonde woman in her late fifties, also waving proudly at Dawson. When the little girl called out a second time, jumping up from her seat, the woman said, "Yes, Daddy did good, but you have to sit down, Savannah."

HE HAD A daughter. Dawson O'Dell had a daughter named Savannah. She had light brown hair and a darling smile that produced deep dimples in her plump cheeks.

Those facts kept circling in Sage's mind as she tried to process the reality of it.

She sat in a daze for the rest of the tie-down competitors. Exactly how old was Savannah? Had Dawson been married *and had a child as well* during those months when he'd slowly won her friendship and eventually her heart? As she considered the possibilities, the steer wrestling event was announced, and she didn't take in much of that either, though she did notice Dawson hazing for their neighbor, Jamie MacCreadie.

Jamie was a few years younger than her, dark haired and intense. His father wasn't too pleased about his rodeo life style, but at least he'd shown up to watch his son perform. His wife, sitting beside him, looked a little overwhelmed, but her face lit up when the announcer called out a time of three point eight seconds for her son.

"Wow, that's world class," Callan said. "Good for Jamie."

"That boy ought to quit playing around at being a rodeo star and go home to help his father on the ranch," was Hawksley's verdict.

Sage didn't let his comment upset her. She already knew that Hawksley valued good ranch workers above rodeo performers. As long as she'd been barrel racing he'd taken *some* interest in her life. But once her world no longer involved horses it had ceased to be relevant to him.

That was okay. She understood that her dad had suffered heartaches in his life that had made him the way he was. And at her age, she no longer needed her father's approval to be happy—although she couldn't deny, it would have been nice.

Next up were the barrel racers and Sage moved forward in her seat, keen to assess the competitors. She'd heard about a woman from Australia—Tegan Ash—but this was her first opportunity to see her in action. Tegan started out well, she was a fearless rider. But she had a little trouble with her foot and almost knocked down the third barrel. It steadied, however, and she ended up with the second best time of the day at 15.95 seconds.

"And that's how they do it Down Under folks," called out the announcer. Tegan, a standout with her blonde hair and bright pink shirt, smiled and waved at the crowd as she rode out of the ring.

"I need a break." Sage stood, stretching out her bum knee.

"Grab us some popcorn?" Dani asked.

"Sure."

She was on her way to the concession stand when a cowboy stepped right in front of her. Her gaze travelled up his dusty jeans, to the checked shirt and his weary smile.

"Nice work, O'Dell," she said acknowledging his success

in the tie-down.

"Thanks. I was happy with it." He looked like he wanted to keep talking, but didn't know what to say.

The smart thing would be for her to keep moving to the concessions. But she couldn't resist asking about the girl in the stands. "So—you have a daughter? I heard her cheering for you."

"Yeah. I noticed you were sitting pretty close to her. For a little thing she sure can be loud."

"Savannah, right?"

He smiled. "Yeah."

That was all he was going to tell her? Suddenly she was so angry she couldn't hold it in anymore. Couldn't pretend what had happened was water under the bridge and that the whole thing meant nothing.

She took a step closer and pressed her fist tight to his chest. "You're awfully quiet all of a sudden, O'Dell. Just tell me this. Were you not only married when we hooked up—did you also have a kid?"

His smile vanished fast, his mouth went hard and his jaw rock firm. Before she knew it he had her fist in his hand and was holding it super tight.

"Savannah was born after. I didn't even know Gina was pregnant."

So many questions spun through her mind. Could she believe him? And why did she still care, so damn much?

"Where's Gina now?"

"In Vancouver. Or maybe Whistler by now. She met a fellow in Canada and followed him over the border."

"She just left her daughter?"

"She sure as hell did—three weeks ago. For the record, it isn't the first time."

"And the woman sitting with Savannah?"

"That's my mother." An uncomfortable look passed over his face. "She's been helping me out with babysitting since Gina took off."

She stared into his face. Was this more lies? Or the truth? She didn't trust herself to tell the difference. She tugged her hand until he finally released it. "That's a heartbreaking story. I'm sure it'll go over well with the ladies at the bar tonight."

A look akin to sadness—or maybe disappointment—washed over his face. "That's a low blow, Sage. Right now I need to say hi to my daughter. She's waiting for me. Can we get a drink later tonight and have a proper discussion?"

Why did she want to say yes? She was such a fool. He seemed sincere and honest right now—but hadn't she thought he had those same qualities five years ago? She'd been so naïve back then. It still made her heart ache when she remembered how easily she'd talked to him. She'd shared so much. Way *too* much.

And now he knew, not just every curve on her body, but also so many of her private thoughts. Lucinda Williams had a song beseeching her ex-lover to please don't tell anybody the secrets that they shared. Boy did Sage ever relate to that song.

All around them were people, everyone moving, heading either to the washrooms or for food, or back to the stands. Sage moved in closer, to keep what she was about to say between the two of them. Now she could see the pores in his tanned skin, the light gold lines in his green eyes, the sun bleached strands in his hair.

"I'm not meeting you for a drink, O'Dell. You are the first cowboy I ever hooked up with. And what you put me through—I was humiliated. Not to mention terrified."

"Aw, Sage."

"No. Let me finish. Can we please just give each other space and get through the weekend? I'm not proud of what happened back then. Being the other woman is definitely not my scene—and I sure don't want my friends and family to find out about it. Is it asking too much for you to respect that?"

His face had been getting paler with each word. Good. Hopefully the message was sinking in.

"My goal sure isn't to make you feel worse, Sage. I was hoping—"

"Don't. There is no room for hoping here."

She tried to walk past Dawson but he kept blocking her. Finally he put his hands on her shoulders and held her still.

He should have looked abashed after the dressing down she'd just given him, but he didn't. Instead he seemed—

shaken.

"I'm so sorry, Darlin'. I am. I thought I was doing the honorable thing not following after you back then. But I guess I should have tracked you down sooner. Ah—hell. There's too much for me to explain to you standing right here. Just give me fifteen minutes. Grey's Saloon. Later tonight, say around nine."

After he left, she couldn't remember what she'd been about to do. Finally someone bumped into her. Some of the beer and popcorn he'd been carrying spilled to the ground.

Popcorn. That was it.

Chapter Three

"HERE'S YOUR POPCORN." Sage handed the two bags down to her sisters and father. Staring at the arena, she tried to focus. It didn't work. "What's happening?" she asked Dani.

"They're loading the horses into the chutes. The saddle bronc riding will start any minute." Dani munched on some popcorn then gave her a studied look. "You were gone a long time."

"Big line," Sage mumbled. She was thinking about the way Dawson had said "Darlin'" A lot of cowboys used the term indiscriminately. But Dawson's version had sounded so tender and sweet.

She couldn't help thinking about the man she'd thought she'd known five years ago. Somehow their schedules had aligned almost perfectly that summer. Rodeo after rodeo she kept bumping into him. They were friends first. He was one of few who had recognized her fear of performing. He started showing up before her events, giving her pep talks. Telling her how good she was.

And she had been good. Technically, very good.

What she'd been missing was the drive to win. All she had was the drive to survive. And her horse had sensed that and it showed in her stats. "I want to quit," she'd once admitted to Dawson. He'd said the last thing she'd expected: "Then why don't you?"

She surprised herself by telling him the truth—she didn't want to disappoint her father. Hawksley had dealt with many setbacks in his life already. She knew how much he wanted this for her. At an early age she'd been singled out as having a talent for barrel racing and her father had been so damn pleased. The only time she remembered him paying her any attention at all, was when he was giving her advice on how to handle a horse, or tips on what to expect from her competitors.

Sage sighed.

Dani bumped her shoulder. "What's wrong?"

There was no way Sage could tell her. And she didn't know why. Dani loved her. She would never judge her harshly—and it would be good to know what a logical, objective person thought about the situation.

But—the words were locked in her heart. And she couldn't even blame Dawson and the horrible history between them. No, this problem went back further, to a door that was closed, that she wasn't supposed to open.

You used to be such a chatterbox.

SAGE DIDN'T HAVE much heart for the rodeo anymore. But her sisters would be disappointed if she took off now. And they'd be full of questions, too. So she decided to sit it out. There were only two events left now, anyway. Saddle bronc and bull riding.

Both Jamie MacCreadie and Dawson were in the lineup for the bronc riding event. But each cowboy's performance was less than stellar. Jamie ended up with a lackluster horse and the opportunity for a re-ride. On the other hand, Dawson's mount was a hell-raiser, but he barely managed to keep his seat.

"What's wrong with that cowboy?" Hawksley sounded disgusted. "He was great at the tie-down. But that horse was in charge from the second they opened the chute."

No one disputed their father's verdict. And Sage wasn't surprised when Dawson earned a score in the mid-seventies. No cowboy would be happy with that, especially not one of Dawson's caliber.

His little girl didn't seem to care. She cheered anyway, and Dawson saluted her with his hat again, though this time he didn't quite manage a smile.

Sage stayed to watch Jamie's re-ride which he totally rocked with a score of 89. She noticed the barrel racer in pink, Tegan Ash from Australia, cheering madly on the sidelines. She could remember the days when she'd cheered just as enthusiastically for Dawson.

The crowds cheered loudest of all for the bull-riding

event—and in particular for legend Colton Thorpe who was the rodeo guest chair this year. Sage was on the edge of her seat for his entire eight-second ride and when it was done, Callan whistled and stomped her feet.

"There is a man who keeps improving with age," Dani said.

"What? You weren't too busy checking his stats to notice?" Callan's gaze fell on the empty seat between them. "Where's Mattie?"

"She went to buy some water, I think," Dani said.

Sage had been so engrossed by the bull-riding she hadn't registered her sister's exit, either. Now she felt badly for not realizing how difficult this event would be for her sister to watch. She leaned over to ask Dani and Callan, "Did Mattie tell you one of Wes's buddies was killed in a bull riding event this June?"

Callan nodded. "I read about it online. Absolutely horrible. Someone even posted a video of the accident on YouTube. I didn't watch it, of course."

"Dreadful," Dani agreed. "I hope Wes will wake up and smell the coffee now. He's too old to be competing in rodeos. Besides, Mattie's been holding down the fort at their ranch long enough. Now that the twins are off to college, it's time he did his share."

"No kidding," Callan agreed. "Mattie's been a saint to put up with Wes all these years."

"Careful," Sage cautioned. She could see Mattie walking

toward the stands with two bottles of water in hand. "Anyway, it's not up to us. Mattie's crazy about Wes and she always has been."

"Stop your gabbing." Their father stood up suddenly.

Sage wondered if he'd heard what they were talking about. Or if he cared. There was no telling by the expression on her father's face, which was as inscrutable as always.

"I want to get to the steak dinner early, while the food is fresh," he continued.

They arrived at the park in front of the Courthouse at five-thirty, well before the official opening, and Callan snagged them a table in a prime position with a good view of the stage. Another band was playing this evening—traditional bluegrass—and Sage could tell the old-timers were especially pleased. They managed to catch the first steaks off the barbecue and ate in relative peace.

But soon old friends and neighbors started showing up and her sisters dispersed in the crowd, chatting and laughing and catching up on news.

Sage was in the line to buy more drink vouchers when old Bill Sheenan joined the queue behind her. Over the years Sage had perfected the art of avoiding the man, but tonight she felt trapped. She immediately turned her back to him and stared dead ahead. She even considered bolting.

But her sisters wanted more wine.

And really, all she had to do was ignore him.

"Hear your chocolate shop's doing well."

Why was he talking to her? Though he was their family's closest neighbor, the long-standing feud between him and her father was reason enough that casual friendly conversations just didn't happen.

"Look Sage, I've always felt bad about what you saw when you were a little girl."

She gasped, then shook her head, signaling that she didn't want him to say another word.

But he persisted. "Did your mother ever explain—?"

He didn't get out another word. Because her father had joined the line, too. And Hawksley's right hook caught the side of Bill's jaw and sent him reeling.

"Fight!" The call was out, and a crowd started to gather.

But Bill didn't strike back. He just stepped up to Hawksley and said something Sage was pretty sure only the three of them could hear.

"That was a long time coming, so I won't retaliate. At least not tonight. But one day you're going to have to answer for what you did to Bev."

Then Bill turned his back and quietly took his leave.

Sage stared at her father. "Why did you hit him?"

Looking into her father's bourbon-colored eyes, she could see the sort of deep rage—and hurt—that didn't come from disputes over water rights. All these years she'd tried to protect her dad from the secret that she worried would destroy him.

But her father knew about the affair.

Had known all along.

Hawksley took her by the elbow and led her away from the crowd, closer to the library.

"What did you see, Sage? What did Bill want to talk to you about?"

She stared mutely at him. She didn't want to hurt him.

"You saw them, didn't you? Your mother and that man."

She had never been able to tell her father an outright lie. "Yes."

She didn't add the details. She'd been eleven, home sick from school, when her mother said she had to run into town but she'd be back in a few hours. If Sage needed anything she should ask Judy, their hired help, who was picking raspberries in the field behind the equipment shed.

Sage had spent the first hour zonked out with fever. But then she started feeling better. And she thought about the vanity table upstairs in her mother's room with all her fancy jewelry and makeup. There were strict rules in their house. The girls were never to enter their parents' room without knocking and waiting for permission first.

But Sage, bored and feeling sorry for herself, climbed the stairs and ignored that rule.

The lock hadn't deterred her. She had a clip in her hair and knew how to use it.

An innocent eleven-year-old had opened that door. And what she saw on the other side had seared her soul. To see her mother in *that* position with her father would have been shocking enough. But with Bill Sheenan!

"Did your mother—talk to you about it?"

She could imagine how awkward this was for him. Her father was a practical man who only spoke about practical matters. This was so far out of his comfort zone that she wasn't surprised he couldn't look her in the eyes. But she could see his throat working, probably swallowing back emotions he didn't want to deal with.

"Not really. She told me to forget what I saw. She said I was too young to understand, and she'd explain when I was older."

But six months later, her mother had been killed while helping her father deliver a calf. And the day for explanations had simply never come.

For all that her father was a gruff man, he rarely swore. He did then, however.

He still had hold of her elbow and his grip tightened, painfully so. "Do your sisters know?"

"I never told..." She almost said "anybody" but that wouldn't have been true. Because back in the days when she'd thought she could trust him, she'd relayed the entire story to Dawson. "I never told them."

"Good. Keep it that way. We don't need to ever refer to this again." Her father released his hold on her then. He dug his hands into his pockets and came up with the keys to the SUV.

"Tell your sisters it's time to go home. I'll drive around

the park and pick them up in front of the old Railway Depot."

"But it's early. They won't want to leave."

"If they want a ride home, they'll leave."

HAVING HEARD ABOUT the fight—or rather, the punch—her sisters decided they'd better go home with Hawksley and make sure he didn't get into any more trouble. It wasn't even seven so Sage figured she might as well go in to work now that the evening had been pretty much ruined.

She was halfway through the crowd when she spotted Dawson sitting at a table with his mother and daughter. He was cutting up some steak for his daughter and she felt a bubble of sweet sorrow, seeing what a devoted father he seemed to be.

He isn't all bad.

No, he wasn't. But she'd always known that. Dawson's numerous good qualities were what made the whole situation between them all the more tragic.

He looked up then and caught her watching them. She tried to hurry away, but he motioned for her to come closer. With his mother and daughter both eyeing her curiously, she didn't see any other option.

"Hi, there. Delicious dinner, isn't it?" She approached his mother, holding out her hand. "I'm Sage Carrigan. I know your son from the circuit. I used to be a barrel-racer."

"Nice to meet you, Sage." The older woman's handshake was limp—she offered only her fingers, not her palm—but her gaze was sharp and Sage could tell that she was being sized-up, woman-to-woman.

"That's my mother Patricia Anderson," Dawson said. "And this is my daughter Savannah."

"Hey there, Savannah. I like your hat."

"Thank you. I like your belt buckle," the little girl replied. "Did you win it? It looks like one my Daddy has. Only smaller."

"Yes I did. It's one of few that I did manage to win. I wasn't as good at the rodeo as your father is."

"And yet, you never saw a finer rider," Dawson said. "Watching Sage on a horse is like seeing a beautiful sunset."

The compliment stunned her. And his mother, as well. Patricia's mouth was actually parted in surprise as she stared from her son to this woman she'd only just met.

"Well… I should be going. Enjoy the rest of your meal. It was nice meeting you both." She smiled at Patricia and then more genuinely at Savannah.

"Hang on a second." Dawson rose quickly from his seat and took her arm, leading her further into the crowd.

She knew she should pull away. But the truth was, it felt wonderful to have him touch her again.

"I thought I saw you in the middle of that skirmish in the ticket line a few minutes ago," Dawson said. "Are you all right? I was on my way to help, when I suddenly couldn't see you anymore."

"I'm fine. That was my father taking a shot at Bill Sheenan."

"That name sounds familiar."

"He owns the ranch next to ours."

Dawson's eyebrows went up. "So he's the one…"

She shook off his hand then, something she should have done sooner. Why was he acting all caring and protective? He had no right. No right at all.

"I've got to go. You should get back to your daughter."

TEN MINUTES LATER Sage was in her store and it had never felt like more of a haven to her. She inhaled deeply as she stepped inside. Chocolate. Was there anything better?

She spelled off Rose Linn, who'd been working with her since the store opened. "I'll take over for tonight, Rose. Thanks. See you tomorrow?"

They usually closed on Sundays but with the rodeo in town they were making an exception.

"Right after I take my folks to church and make them some lunch," Rose promised. Though she was only twenty-four herself, Rose always spoke about her elderly parents as if they were her children.

"By the way," Rose added, "Your cousin Eliza dropped in, hoping to talk to you. She asked if you could drop by the B & B sometime."

"Did she say what she wanted?" A visit from Eliza Bramble was unusual. Ever since she'd moved to Marietta two years ago, she'd been somewhat of a hermit, refusing all invitations to the Circle C and showing no interest in getting to know the Carrigan side of her family.

Callan figured Eliza was after the Bramble House, worming her way into great aunt Mabel's favor so she would inherit when the old lady died. As far as Sage was concerned, anyone who could put up with Mabel deserved the house.

But there were rumors that a large sum of money was part of the inheritance.

And if that were the case, Dani felt it was only fair that all the Bramble cousins share in the family wealth.

Sage had no idea how many cousins there actually were. Most of the Brambles had long since moved away, most of them to California. Only Sage's mother, and great aunt Mable, had remained.

As Rose was leaving the store, Jamie MacCreadie was coming in. He removed his hat and nodded at Rose, then at Sage.

"Hey, Jamie. I saw you had a good day at the rodeo. Lucky thing you took that re-ride."

"Thanks Sage. You ever miss being a competitor?"

"Honestly? No." She shuddered. "I wouldn't risk it with my bum knee, anyway. That Australian rider looked good. A special friend?" Since she'd known Jamie most of her life, she felt she could tease him a little.

But her comment hit the mark a little harder than intended. His face reddened and he stared down at his boots. "Tell you the truth, I'm not too sure. One minute she's driving me crazy. The next she's doing the exact same thing—but in an entirely different way."

"Sorry to break the news, Jamie. But you've got it bad."

"Ya think?" He managed a one sided grin. "Wondered if I could score some points if I bought her some chocolate?"

"A *much* better choice over flowers," she assured him, with a silent apology to Risa, the nice new owner of the florist shop next door. They hadn't had a chance to get to know one another yet, but Sage was hoping they would become friends. "How about I pick out some of my favorites for you? I'll package them in a pretty box with lots of ribbon."

He seemed relieved that she'd offered. When she was done she had to ask him about his hair, the dark ends curling up at his shirt collar. "What is it with you cowboys? How come you never get your hair cut properly?"

He grinned, his mood restored somehow now that he had a gift to give his lady.

"Girls like us rough, Sage. What can I say?"

She had a few more customers after Jamie left. Enough so she felt justified in having kept the store open a few hours longer than usual. By the time she'd closed up, it was nine.

She wondered if Dawson was at Grey's Saloon, waiting for her, even though she hadn't agreed to meet him there.

This afternoon he'd sure seemed anxious to tell her the whole sordid story of his marriage.

But what was the point? Words couldn't alter the facts. And spending more time with him could prove dangerous to her peace of mind.

She'd been in love with him then, and those feelings were already stirring inside her again. There was only one more day of rodeo, but she still had to protect herself. If Gina had taken off with another guy three weeks ago, that meant she and Dawson were still legally married.

This time Sage knew the score so there would be no excuse if she fell for him again.

Especially since there was a child involved.

Chapter Four

THE NEXT AFTERNOON, Sage sat through the rodeo finals with her sisters, wearing her cowboy hat low and sticking close to family. Her father hadn't come today.

"He's in the most god-awful mood," Dani complained. "What happened between him and Bill Sheenan last night? We heard he actually threw a punch."

"And Bill didn't retaliate," Mattie added. "Doesn't that seem strange?"

"Oh, you know. The old feud." Sage dipped her hat lower, slunk down in her seat.

"There had to more to it than that." Callan was harder to fool than the others because she knew their dad the best.

Sage had promised her father that she would keep their mother's affair secret from her sisters, and in her heart she felt it was the right thing to do. That way their memories of mom could remain unsullied. But the end result was that they were harder on their father than he deserved.

No matter how tough and sometimes cold he could seem, Sage was always able to remind herself that he'd been hurt by the one person who should have loved him the most. Now that she knew he'd been aware of the affair, she felt even more sorry for him.

Though Hawksley would hate that—he wasn't one to accept pity from anyone, least of all one of his daughters.

Sage often wondered if her father would have been different if he'd had a son. Maybe some of the pressure would have come off her and her sisters. She certainly remembered his reaction when Callan had been born, though she had been only four at the time.

"Another damn girl."

That's what they'd been to him. One damn girl after another. And yet their mother had assured them all that he didn't mean it. "Your father loves you. He just has a strange way of showing it."

The cowboys put on a good show that afternoon, not that Sage was in a mood to appreciate it.

The feisty cowgirl from Australia won the barrel-racing. Jamie, cheering on the sidelines, looked thrilled.

Sage purposefully stared down at the program when it was Dawson's turn at the tie-down event and later riding the bucking horses. She could tell how well he was doing by the roar of the crowd, though, and his scores were high. Probably high enough that he would earn all-around and the big prize money.

Well good for him. He could take his money and move on to the next town and the next rodeo. Hopefully by now he realized coming to Marietta had been a mistake.

If he'd wanted to say he was sorry a nice Hallmark card in the mail would have done the trick.

MONDAY MORNING SAGE got on her bike a little earlier than usual so she could stop by the Bramble House on her way to work. She was looking forward to returning to routine. They'd had a farewell dinner at the Circle C last night and she'd promised Dani she'd come to visit her in Seattle this December to do some Christmas shopping. She'd given Mattie an extra big hug. Somehow the weekend had whizzed by and the two of them hadn't had a chance to have a proper talk.

She'd wanted to hear more about Wes, and how the girls were doing at college and whether Mattie was coping okay with her empty nest.

But she'd had to content herself with telling her big sister, "You're beautiful, Matt. Inside and out."

"What's with the sappy goodbyes? You all live in the same state for heaven's sake," Dani had pointed out in her logical way.

Which was true, since Bishop Stables—where Mattie and Wes bred and trained Tennessee Walking Horses—was just north of Missoula. Still, the drive was over three hours long and in reality Sage didn't visit with Mattie any more often than with Dani.

Sage rounded a corner on her bike and turned right onto Bramble Lane. Changing gears as the grade shifted, she took a moment to appreciate the rich golden-colored leaves on the willows along the river. Soon those branches would be bare. If only autumn wasn't such a fleeting season. Why couldn't it drag on and on the way the winter always did?

There were so many beautiful homes on this street. Displays of red and gold chrysanthemums and fat, orange pumpkins graced many of the porches in a tribute to fall. Sage slowed as she neared the house of her dreams. She'd coveted it so badly she'd actually phoned the realtor, Tod Styles, to inquire about the asking price.

She hadn't been happy about potentially giving a commission to Tod, because he'd been a real jerk to her friend Chelsea a while back. But when she'd found out how much they were asking for the house, it no longer mattered. The house at 34 Bramble Lane was out of her league.

She knew the owners had already left town, so when she spotted two vehicles in the drive—one a dusty black truck, the other Tod's pristine red Lexus, she braked hard. Two men were in the front yard chatting.

One was Tod.

And damned if the other wasn't Dawson O'Dell.

He noticed her about the same moment she spotted him. "Hang on a minute, Tod."

Tod glanced over his shoulder, and recognizing Sage, gave her a cool nod. "Sure thing. I'll just make that call."

Tod gave her another look, actually a frown, then climbed into the front seat of his car with his phone in hand.

Meanwhile Dawson was still moving toward her. She could tell his body was hurting, but he was still gorgeous. It was there in the deceptively lazy way he moved his long lean body. The fall of his hair across his forehead. The knowing spark in the mossy green of his eyes.

"What are you doing here?" she asked.

"What does it look like? I'm buying a house."

"But—you can't!" Shock made her say that—even though it was clearly an illogical comment and Dani, if she were here, would be the first to point it out.

"It's not like a wedding. You don't get to stand up and voice your objections." He tilted his head to one side. "By the way the helmet's a good look. Love what it does for your cheekbones."

She resisted the urge to remove the helmet and fluff up her hair. So she looked crappy. That didn't matter. What mattered was that Dawson wasn't just in town for the rodeo. He was buying a house. "Why didn't you tell me you're planning to move here?"

"Honestly? I was hoping we could get to a friendly footing before I mentioned it."

"A friendly footing." Was he insane?

"So do you like the house?" he asked. "What do you think of the neighborhood?"

No way was she going to admit to him that she absolutely *loved* it. "It's okay, I guess."

"You think Savannah will be happy here? She'll be starting school full time next year. I'm going to register her in kindergarten as soon as we get settled."

Was he trying to imply that the reason he was buying this house was for his daughter's sake? But he could have purchased a house in any one of a hundred different towns he'd been to in his travels. Why had he picked *her* town?

"Dawson, honey? Are you still busy?" His mother emerged from the side of the house, holding Savannah's hand. "The back yard is wonderful. I was just giving our pumpkin a ride on the tire swing. She didn't want to stop."

As soon as the little girl saw her father she ran for him. He swung her up into his arms and she gave him a kiss, then looked at Sage.

"Hi. Where are you going?"

"To work." Sage tried to smile, even though she was still feeling so angry.

"Sage owns the chocolate shop where I bought you that treat the other day."

"Ohhhh." Savannah's eyes—the same shape and shade of green as her father's, so no question about *her* paternity—were big and round. Sage realized she'd just gone up a few notches in the little girl's esteem.

But not his mother's. Patricia had her hands on her slender hips. She was dressed in a linen shift dress and heels—rather much for Monday morning in a small, western town.

"Well. It's, Sage, isn't it? Don't you look sporty."

"Just on my way to work, when I noticed all the activity. This house has been vacant for a long time." Hopefully the implication was that there was a reason it hadn't been sold.

Tod stepped out of his car then, tucking his phone into the breast pocket of his suit as he walked toward them. "Just spoke to the seller. They're fine with next Friday as the closing date." He nodded at Sage. "If you've come to ask about the house again, it's sold. The financing condition was just lifted."

Dawson gave her a quick, surprised look. And Sage felt like trying out her father's right hook on Tod. She did not want Dawson knowing that she'd had her eye on this house, too. But big-mouthed Tod had just blown it.

"It's a great house. Congratulations Dawson. I'm sure you and Savannah will be very happy here." If she sounded less than enthused, well, she couldn't help it.

"Don't forget Grandma," Patricia added in a chipper voice. "Someone has to look after our little pumpkin when Daddy's working."

"I've got a line on a day-care, Mom. And some sitters with flexible hours when I'm on nights."

"Why bother with all that when I'm right here, ready and available. Doesn't your new job start next Monday?"

Sage raised her eyebrows. Sounded like she had another surprise in store. "New job?" she asked, looking directly at Dawson.

"Law enforcement," he elaborated, not too helpfully.

Patricia smiled proudly. "He's going to be the new deputy. Sheriff Toby Walton offered him the position last month."

SAGE'S MIND WAS still numb with shock when she coasted up to Bramble House thirty seconds later. She pushed her bike up the sweeping walk-way. Weeds had poked through the cracks in the concrete. Taking a closer than usual look at the Victorian mansion, she realized the white trim needed painting, too.

Maybe Great Aunt Mabel wasn't as rich as her sisters thought.

She propped her bike against the steps, hesitated, then removed her helmet and shook out her hair.

Dawson's mother's comment still resonated...*Don't you look sporty.* It clearly hadn't been meant as a compliment.

Eliza opened the front door before Sage had a chance to knock. Her cousin, who had moved to Marietta after her fiancé died in a hiking accident in Glacier National Park, was a tall, thin, *sporty-looking*—as Dawson's mother would say—woman of thirty-two. Before the accident Eliza and her finance had worked for a big insurance firm in California, which was where her parents and siblings still lived.

She had short, dark curly hair, serious brown eyes, and lips that had a tendency to look stern—maybe because they were so thin, and Eliza rarely smiled.

She wasn't smiling now, though she did give an approving nod. "Thanks for coming. Do you have time for coffee?"

Sage hadn't expected the invitation. If she accepted, she was going to be late opening the store. Yet, this was the first friendly overture Eliza had made. "Sure."

She stepped into a large foyer papered in a brown, rose and cream floral pattern. The wooden floors gleamed in the morning light and wide French doors led to an adjacent sitting room—one Sage remembered well from previous visits.

This room was papered, as well, and outfitted with dark antiques, most of which were covered with knick-knacks. A handsome fireplace rescued the room from appearing too feminine. And the brown leather furniture arranged around it, Sage already knew, was as comfortable as it looked.

Sage sank into the sofa in her usual spot.

Great Aunt Mabel was to her left, in an upright arm chair. With her hair in a bun, complete with hair net, and her perfect posture, she looked like an aging ballet instructor. But as far as Sage knew, her aunt hadn't worked a day in her life.

"Hello, Aunt Mabel. How are you?"

"Fine, Sage. And your family?"

While they exchanged pleasantries, Eliza poured coffee from a silver urn, into Royal Albert cups, the same pattern as Sage's mother's. Which made Sage wonder if her mother's china was perhaps more valuable than any of them had guessed.

Too bad the gold trim had all but been erased by the dishwasher…

"You must have been busy for the rodeo," Sage said, though the place had a quiet, empty feeling now.

"The last guest left half an hour ago." Eliza looked like this suited her just fine.

"My father would roll in his grave if he knew we were accepting common guests into this house."

It was a rant Sage had heard before from her great aunt. But what surprised her was that people were willing to pay money to stay in a home where their presence was so clearly resented.

"The reason I wanted to talk to you—" Eliza was ready to get to the point. "Is because I was hoping you and your sisters would help me with my new project."

"Oh?"

"Eliza's going to write a book on the Bramble family history," Great Aunt Mabel announced with pride. "About time someone did it."

"I've gone through all the old family letters and diaries," Eliza said.

"And she's researched on that Web thing, too."

"She means the Internet, of course. I've traced our family tree back to the fifteen hundreds. But in the book I plan to focus on the Montana years. What brought our family out here and how we all but built the town of Marietta."

Sage's gaze went to the family photographs hanging in silver frames next to the fireplace. When she was little, her mother had explained who was who, but Sage could no longer remember. What she did recall was her mother's pride when she'd explained that the Brambles were one of the town's founding families. Her great-great grandfather had been a prominent journalist as well as a mining engineer.

Sage doubted, however, that the credit rested *entirely* with them.

"We were hoping," Eliza continued, "That you would check your mother's papers to see if she had anything that would help with this project."

Steven and Cordelia Bramble hadn't been impressed when their eldest daughter elected to marry a simple local rancher. His lack of education and social prominence had been liabilities that no amount of land or money could overcome. After her marriage, Beverly had rarely seen her parents, and it was only after their deaths that she'd been invited back to the family home by her father's unmarried sister, Mable.

"You think Mom took important family documents with her when she married dad?"

"Possibly." Eliza shrugged. "Anything pertaining to the family would be interesting,"

"I'll try. But I can't make any promises."

SALES WERE OFTEN slow on Monday and today they seemed especially so. Maybe it was a good thing. Between her weird conversation with Mabel and Eliza that morning, and the revelation that Dawson had found a job in Marietta and was buying a house, Sage was having a hard time concentrating.

When Rose showed up for her afternoon shift, she glanced at the balance on the till and sighed. "Rodeo hangover. I think it's hit the entire town. Hardly anyone out on the streets today. Sure you want me to stay?"

Sage knew that Rose counted on every hour she could give her. "Yes. You can watch over the showroom while I start a new batch of chocolate in the kitchen."

Having a job to focus on was helpful. Otherwise she'd surely go insane imagining Dawson moving into her beautiful little house with the pretty red door. Not to mention going to work for the Sheriff's Department.

She wondered if anyone had told him… ? No, probably not.

The buzzer on the roaster sounded. It was time to put in the next batch. She'd done a lot of experimenting over the years, and had settled on a long, low roasting process to get the maximum flavor from her premium cacao beans.

Tomorrow she'd crack the beans into nibs then use a blower a lot like a hairdryer to remove the husks. The process of making a fresh batch of chocolate took the best part of a week. The slowest step was the conching and refining which usually required about thirty hours, all told.

The rest of the day went by quickly and Sage was surprised when Rose stuck her head in the door, tossing her apron in the laundry basket. "It's almost six and I haven't had a customer in an hour. Mind if I head home ten minutes early?"

"Go ahead. I'm almost done here. Put up the Closed sign on your way out, would you?"

"Sure. See you on Friday."

Rose worked Friday, Saturday and Monday, a schedule that coordinated best with her parents' needs. Sage's other part-time employee, Dakota, came in afternoons on Tuesday, Wednesday and Thursday. Mostly Sage worked a full six-day week. But having the extra help meant she could slip out when she needed to.

Sage switched off all her equipment before turning out the lights and tossing her own apron in the basket. She'd make a final check of the storefront, before leaving from the back where she kept her bike.

"Long day?" Dawson asked. He was standing behind the counter, studying the chocolate-making photographs. Her friends Jenny and Chelsea had taken them for her, then helped her select the right dark frame to set them off nicely against the pale coffee-colored walls.

"How did you get in?" She'd been in a state of mild shock ever since this morning. It had been one thing knowing she had to deal with three days of him being in the same town as her. But now it seemed as if his move was permanent.

And she honestly didn't know if she could handle that.

"I caught Rose as she was leaving. Told her I was a good friend. Isn't it nice how people in small towns are so trusting?"

She glanced at the sign in the window. Her side read Open, which meant to the world, she was closed. Next she tried the door. Locked.

"Why are you doing this?"

"Because you didn't meet me for a drink the other night. And I know you'll keep putting me off if I give you the chance."

She couldn't argue with that. What he was saying was absolutely true.

"Sage, Darlin', I think it's high time we did some talking.

Chapter Five

DAWSON WAS STARTING to feel like a stalker and he hated that. He'd been dreaming of seeing Sage again for so long, but their reunion wasn't working out the way he'd imagined. Not even close. He'd had so much to work out, to plan and organize. He supposed it was only to be expected that something would get screwed up.

She brought out a second chair from the back and sat on the other side of the counter from him. "Well? What is it you want off your chest?"

He rubbed his eyes. It had been a long three days. But Sage—she looked gorgeous. He wondered, did she ever think about all the things that had gone right between them—before they'd gone so horribly wrong?

"There's a lot I want to say. How about I open with this. When I invited you to my trailer, I did it because I loved you. I didn't know Gina followed me to Wyoming. And I sure as hell didn't know she owned a shotgun." He brushed his hair back from his forehead and let out a long breath. "It wasn't loaded, by the way."

"That would have been nice to know *then*."

"Were you really afraid she was going to shoot you?"

"Of course I was afraid! Weren't you?"

"Hell, no. Gina's mostly bluster, just the way her hair is mostly hair spray and air."

"If you think I find it comforting that I was scared out of my mind and you weren't, here's a news flash. I don't."

She was mad, and he got that. But he couldn't look at her without remembering how amazing it had felt to make love to her. The connection between them had worked on every level. And it was something he'd never experienced before in his life.

"You wanted to talk. So why so quiet?"

"I know I should have told you about Gina before things got… romantic between us."

Sage turned away from him, for a moment. Then, her voice quiet, she asked, "Why didn't you?"

"I was embarrassed, I guess. I'd made a big mistake and I didn't want to admit it." He hated looking back on those days. But it was full disclosure time. "I met Gina shortly after I'd attended my mother's sixth wedding." He heard the disdain in his voice, and could tell Sage did, too. He was sorry for that. Generally he tried not to judge his mother. But he didn't find it easy.

"Did you meet Gina at a rodeo?"

"Sort of. In a bar, after. She was wild in a dancing on table tops with a wet T-shirt sort of way, and I was at a stage in my life when I thought her lack of inhibitions was a good thing. We ended up getting married in Reno two months later. And I guess we had about three or four pretty good months. But we also had some whopping fights and soon we were fighting all the time. That was when I came to the sorry realization that I was following in my mother's footsteps and that I was done with Wife Number One."

Sage looked horrified. "That sounds so cynical."

"To you, sure. But given the way I'd grown up, it just seemed to be the way the world worked. Gina and I were off and on for a few more months. Then we had a big fight up at Fort Benton in Montana. She tossed our rings in the Missouri River and told me the next word would be coming from her lawyer. I said 'fine with me, please make it quick,' and went back on the road."

"To another rodeo..." Sage said softly.

"Sure. Rodeo was my life. And I knew Gina wasn't. Stupidly, I took Gina at her word when she said she'd be contacting a lawyer. I wish like hell that I'd gone to a lawyer on my own."

Sage shook her head, clearly wishing the same thing. "And how much later did you and I meet?"

"A few months. You knew I was following you, right?" He'd find out which rodeo she was heading to next, then register right behind her.

"I suspected." She pulled back a little. But she didn't look upset.

Their romance had started slow. Rather than going to the bar after the rodeo, Sage liked to get on her mountain bike and check out the local trails.

He'd bought a bike too and got hooked on the sport as well.

Later, they'd grab a meal, then find a coffee shop that stayed open late and talk until midnight. By the time they'd made love he'd known for certain that this was the girl he wanted to spend his life with. Wife Number Forever.

But then his past had bit him in the butt.

That seemed to be the way things went for guys like him.

"When it was good between us, it was damn near perfect, wasn't it?"

Sage crossed her arms. "I thought so at the time. But I was wrong."

"So now we're back where we started?"

She nodded. "You were married and you should have told me. You had to know it would matter."

He swallowed, miserably aware what she was referring to. "Because of what happened with your Mom."

"Yes."

DAWSON WAS THE only person she'd ever told about the locked door and what was behind it. In some ways for her, sharing that secret had been even more intimate than sharing her body.

Her Mom hadn't meant it to happen, but what she'd seen that day had stolen her childhood. Nothing was what she'd believed it to be. Her mother didn't love her father. Did she even love them, her children?

Sage had spent the next six months wondering when her mother was going to leave.

Never guessing it would be a stupid accident with a cow, not Bill Sheenan, that would take her away.

"You're right," Dawson said. "I should have known and I should have said something. But I couldn't stand the idea of you thinking badly of me."

So he'd covered up one mistake with another—a lie.

"What happened with Gina after I left? You two reconciled, I guess."

"Hell, no!"

"But you scratched both your events that afternoon." And he hadn't been there to give her a pep talk before her turn at the barrel-races, either. She sure could have used one. She'd been so shaken up from the confrontation that morning, she shouldn't even have tried to ride.

But she had.

"I didn't go because right after you left Gina told me—well she didn't need to tell me, I could see—that she was pregnant. And I was the father."

"Are you kidding?" She certainly hadn't noticed any such thing. "Gina was pregnant when she was pointing that gun at us?"

"Hell, yeah. Seven months."

"All I saw was that gun—and her hair," Sage admitted.

"Well, she was wearing a loose dress, but she was definitely pregnant and believe me, that was not a complication I was happy about."

Talk about lousy timing. And yet…"That complication led to your daughter."

He tilted his head, acknowledging her point. "Yeah. And that kid is worth all the bad times, she really is. But I won't say the past five years were easy for me."

Sage wondered if those years would have been easier for her, if she'd known the whole story. It was hard to say. "You still could have come round to say good-bye."

"You have no idea how intense things were with Gina. I didn't even believe her at first when she said I was the baby's father. We had the biggest fight ever. And then she threatened to hurt herself—and the baby. That's when Jamie sent me a text and told me you'd had a fall and had been taken to the hospital."

She glanced away.

"I should have been there for you," he said. "And believe me, I wanted to be. But I couldn't just abandon Gina."

"The fall was *my* fault," honesty made her admit. "I knew I should have scratched. I was literally shaking in my boots."

"Aw, Sage. I'm so sorry." He rubbed the side of his face, looking miserable. "Tell me what happened? How did you have the accident?"

The tone of his voice, so gentle and caring, made her want to answer. It was why they had become friends in the first place and why she'd fallen for him so hard. "Coffee Girl and I started okay, but as we were going around the second barrel I miscued her and she slipped and fell. I jumped off, just in time, but landed badly. At the hospital I was told I'd snapped my ACL, sprained my knee and torn the meniscus."

Dawson cringed. "Bet that hurt like hell."

"It wasn't so bad."

"By the next day I had Gina calmed down. I told her I would look after her while she was pregnant and then later I'd support her and the baby. I still wanted a divorce but I didn't push it then. By the next day she was stable enough that I was able to slip away and come to the hospital. But they told me you were gone."

"I still don't know how my father got there so fast. I guess Jamie called him right away with the news and he must have jumped in his truck and driven all night."

"I wish he hadn't."

"You think things would have turned out any different? Gina was still your wife. And she was still pregnant." Sage pushed back from the counter and left her chair. This talk was supposed to be clearing things up, but instead she was more mixed up than ever.

"In some ways the accident was a blessing. Finally I got the nerve to tell my father I didn't want to barrel-race anymore. And you and I were already over by then."

"I didn't want to be," he insisted.

She headed to the far corner. "I'm not sure this talk was a good idea. It doesn't change anything."

He followed after her, blocking her with his wide shoulders, then putting his arms around her. She didn't return the hug, but she didn't fight it either. She'd forgotten how tough and hard he was. He didn't have a body builder's bulk, but there wasn't a soft spot on him.

"Why did you come here?" She didn't need to speak above a whisper since he was holding her so close.

"I had to," was his simple answer.

And then he lifted her chin and when their eyes met, she knew he was going to kiss her.

Her body reacted fast—turning hot, smooth and sweet, like tempered chocolate. She'd wanted this from the first moment she'd seen him. Why was it only Dawson O'Dell who made her feel this way?

At the very last minute she lowered her eyes and turned her head. "Are you still married to her?"

His body tensed and he dropped his arms. "The divorce is in process…"

She held up a hand. Five years later, and the divorce was still in process? "I can't believe this!" Finally she gave him a tired, disappointed look. "You better leave, Dawson. Just go."

OUT ON THE street, Dawson wanted to howl with disappointment. To think there'd been a moment when he'd actually been holding her in his arms. It had felt so right. She smelled of cocoa and vanilla and her beautiful red hair had been so soft against his arms. And now everything was sideways again. And once more it was his fault.

He'd rushed forward, when he should have hung back.

But he'd already waited so damn long.

The birth of Savannah had really sparked the beginning of the process. Looking at her delicate face, he'd decided to change his life for her. But it hadn't been just for his daughter, it had been for Sage as well.

Because for years now when he went to bed at night all he could think about was a beautiful red-head who was so damned afraid of barrel-racing, yet was gutsy enough to go out and do it anyway, week after week.

He'd learned a lot from Sage. Not just about bravery and persistence. She'd told him so many stories about her family and life on their ranch. He'd hung on ever word. She didn't know it, but she'd helped him understand that there were other ways to live than the path he was on.

But wanting to change, and actually making it happen, were two different things.

He'd started being careful with money, saving and putting aside as much as he could. He'd cut out all the drinking and partying and registered for night classes. He was aiming for a different job. A stable life. A divorce from Gina. And a new start with Sage.

He'd managed to achieve the first two.

But the third was a lot more difficult. And the fourth was looking impossible.

"DADDY, WHEN IS Mom coming back?" Savannah was coloring at the built-in table of the trailer. Dawson loved watching her. She curled her entire body over the project, concentrating on filling the spaces just so. His daughter was a perfectionist with everything she did, and he didn't know if that was just her nature, or the way she coped with the constantly changing patterns and routines in her life.

"I'm not sure. We'll ask her next time she calls." When that would be, he had no idea. Her wandering ways were fine with him. He was thrilled to have sole custody of his daughter and more than willing to be generous with visitation rights when Gina bothered to come around.

"Okay." Savannah seemed fine with that, too, thank goodness.

She kept coloring, while he shaved at the bathroom sink with the door open so they could talk.

Savannah liked to talk to him a lot.

Once Sage had liked talking to him as well. So many nights they'd stayed up late and he'd listened to her stories about growing up on the Circle C and had marveled at the vast differences between the two of them.

From the beginning he'd worried that those differences might be too vast to bridge.

And now, the nervous twinges in his gut were saying the same thing. He'd moved to her town, but Sage was more remote than ever.

"Daddy, when are we going to the next rodeo?"

Job done, he rinsed off his razor and zipped it up in his leather tote bag. Savannah was too smart to play with it, but no sense taking chances. "No more rodeos, remember?"

"Oh. Right."

He'd explained so many times, but maybe she didn't believe him. Or maybe she just couldn't imagine staying in one town and not moving all the time. "I'm working for the Sheriff's Office now. And pretty soon, you'll be starting school and we'll be living in that nice house we checked out yesterday."

Savannah pressed a crayon against her cheek as she pondered this. "Is Grandma coming, too?"

He finished buttoning the shirt of his new uniform. "Would you like her to?"

Savannah sighed. "I don't care, Daddy."

She sounded so exasperated. So adult-like. God, this girl of his could make him smile.

"Well, I'm all ready for work. How do I look?"

Savannah studied him, clearly not impressed. "Like the man who gave Mom that ticket. Is that what you do at work, Daddy? Give people tickets if they drive too fast?"

"Yup. That's me. So don't you go driving too fast young lady or you are going to be very sorry."

She gave him her little, worldly smile. "You're being silly. I don't drive."

Not now. One day she would. Dawson was glad that day was far in the future.

"Ready to go for breakfast?" They were going to meet his mother in the diner across from the hotel where she was staying. Patricia would be watching Savannah while he worked his first shift.

He and his mother didn't normally have much to do with one another, but she'd happened to call the day after Gina took off with her new fellow. Turned out husband number six had died a month ago.

His mother wasn't used to being on her own. Usually before each divorce she had her next prospect all lined up.

"You know, honey," she'd told him. "I'm giving up on marriage. It never seems to work out for me."

"Maybe seventh time will be the charm?"

"I doubt it," she said, not catching the sarcasm. "Where did you say you are right now?"

Like a fool, he'd gone and told her.

"I'm going to get in my car and drive there. With Gina gone, you need someone to look after my granddaughter."

Never mind that he'd been doing just fine so far. Patricia needed a project, and lucky them, they were it. Since her arrival, she'd been sticking tight and talking about making the arrangement permanent.

A very scary thought.

He'd already ordered Savannah pancakes and eggs and bacon for himself, when Patricia made her entrance. She never went anywhere without styling her hair and putting on make-up. And wearing heels. Even though she was almost sixty, most of the males in the room kept an eye on her as she sauntered to their booth.

"Good morning! I hope everyone slept well." She slid into the seat next to her granddaughter. When the server came by to fill her coffee cup, she asked for toast—not buttered.

His mother looked a lot like Joni Mitchell had when she'd been in her late fifties. Patricia could sing, too, but she didn't have Joni's famous three octave range. His mother stuck to the lower, sultry notes and when she was younger had performed in bars with various bands. But she'd never been foolish enough to hook up with one of the musicians.

No, she'd looked for the rich, older men in the crowd. And picked them.

"So what should Savannah and I do while you're at work today, honey?"

Dawson took a sip of his coffee and wondered why she would never just use his given name. A thirty-two-year-old man did not really having his mother call him "honey" all the time. He could tell he and his mom had spent too much time together when stuff like this started to drive him crazy.

"Play in the park? Maybe you could take Savannah shopping for some new school clothes." He pulled out his wallet.

"Put that away. Shopping is a great idea. I'd love to treat Savannah to a few new things. Doesn't that sound fun, pumpkin?"

He was honey. His daughter was pumpkin. Dawson held his tongue by taking another drink of coffee.

"Maybe later I could do some shopping for the new house," Patricia continued, moving aside her cup as the server came with their orders. She arched her brows at the sight of Savannah's pancakes with fresh fruit and whipped cream. "My, the calories. Enjoy them while you're young, pumpkin."

"Mom doesn't like calories, either," Savannah said in a very matter-of-fact voice. "I think they're delicious."

Score another one for his daughter. Dawson concentrated on his own breakfast, next, finishing fast, his eye on the time. When he was done, he kissed his daughter's cheek, then thanked his mother for taking care of her.

"Go ahead and shop for clothes, but leave the house stuff for me, Mom. I've got it covered."

"You've never bought a house before, honey. You have no idea how many things you need."

"I'll figure it out." Putting on his hat, he went out to his truck.

He knew Patricia was probably going to ignore him and buy for the new house anyway. But he'd make her return it all. If he let her feather the nest, she was going to want to move in.

And that wasn't happening.

DEPUTY SCOTT BLIVEN had a boyish, eager appearance, belying his ten years' experience on the job. He raked his hand through his dark hair and his eyes brightened when Sheriff Walton assigned him to partner up with Dawson. "Show O'Dell the ropes," Walton instructed, and Dawson nodded his agreement with the plan, even though he suspected he'd seen a lot more ropes when he was rodeoing than he was going to see as the newest deputy.

As the new hire, with no experience, Dawson ought to have been low man on the totem pole. But his standing with the CPRA, and his recent win that weekend, had accorded him a certain measure of respect.

In fact Scott, who was supposed to be touring him around the detachment, started out with more questions than answers.

"So what's up with Trevor Brazile?"

"He's the real deal," Dawson said.

"You ever go out drinking with him? What's he *really* like?"

"I've got a five-year old daughter. I don't do much drinking anymore."

Bliven seemed disappointed to hear that. "Well," he finally said. "You still must have lots of stories."

"Yup." And Dawson was going to make him work for each one of them. Because he wasn't in the mood for looking back. He was a deputy now and he intended to make a success of it.

After the tour was done and Dawson had been introduced to some of the key people, Bliven snagged a set of keys to one of the dark gray SUVs that were used for patrolling. "Thought we'd take the 89 south of town today, show you where we have some of the bigger ranches in the county. Believe it or not, we still have problems with rustlers, and this is one of the areas we need to keep a close watch on."

"Good idea. Think maybe I should drive today? I'll probably get to know the countryside a little faster that way."

It was bull, but Bliven didn't challenge him. Dawson had already pegged the young man as someone who wanted his approval. Not that he intended to take too much advantage of the fact. But he'd been on the road since he was sixteen years old and he had no interest in being a passenger.

It felt good to be in the driver's seat of the silver SUV, a fine set of wheels much nicer than the old pickup he'd been driving for the past eight years. He figured he was better off saving his money for a house, than trading up his vehicle every few years like a lot of his buddies.

As they headed south through the valley, they passed a rancher using a big machine to load hay, no doubt hauling it closer to home in preparation for the snows to come. The autumn colors were still vibrant—patches of gold studded the green of the mountains, and the willows and brush along the river were still orange and yellow. There was a cool snap to the air, and once he'd accelerated to highway speed, Dawson rolled up his window.

He'd seen a lot of places in his travels, but the country around Marietta was among the most beautiful he could remember.

"You lived here long?" he asked his new partner.

"All my life. Except for the years I went to college in Bozeman."

Quite the world traveler. Dawson couldn't help feeling a twinge of jealousy though. He'd never had roots like that. Well, he'd do better by Savannah.

"We just passed the MacCreadie place," Scott said. "Tucked back in that valley"—he pointed—"is the Douglases place. Back in '97 someone broke into the home at night and murdered the husband and wife and a couple of the younger kids. Two older boys survived."

Dawson shook his head. Hard to believe such an ugly thing had happened in this place of amazing beauty. "Who did it?"

"Unsolved, to this day." Bliven paused, then continued with his commentary. "Now we're coming to Sheenan land. They own thousands of acres—as do the MacCreadies and the Carrigans. Must be nice, huh?"

"Must be." He knew a lot about horses and quite a bit

about calves and bulls, but Dawson had never actually worked on a ranch. All he had to go on were the stories Sage had shared.

"Mattie, Callan and I loved the lifestyle. Mom and Dani never did. Dad expected everyone to pitch in, though, and so we all did."

He could remember the night she'd told him that. They'd been in Oakdale, California, mid-March. He hadn't been in love with her yet. Or maybe he had, but just didn't realize it. She'd been wearing her thick red hair in a braid that fell over one shoulder.

All that day he'd had to fight the urge to touch it.

Unlike most redheads, Sage had milky skin, and usually she wore a hat to block the sun. He'd never seen a cowgirl who could wear a hat like Sage. She put it on her head, and she owned it. "I can dress the part," she'd once told him, when she'd been all decked out in the light blue colors she wore for competing. "But it's the performing that scares me."

"…and this here is the creek that divides the Sheenans from the Carrigans. You can see their big ranch house over this rise. Nice, huh?"

Scott must have been talking all this time, but Dawson had no idea what he'd said before the name Carrigan made him snap to attention. He looked for the house and saw a long, ranch-style home tucked into a grove of pine. Beyond the main house was a compound of impressive outbuildings, painted white with green roofs.

Had Sage really grown up here?

"When you say Carrigan—is that Hawksley Carrigan?"

"None other." Bliven pushed his hat up higher on his forehead. "You've heard of him?"

Dawson kept his tone cool. Casual. "One of his daughters was a barrel racer. We met a few years back."

"Ah. You're talking about Sage. She's the second youngest of his four daughters. They're all lookers. But she's the only redhead. Pretty and rich besides. We all gave Walton a hard time when they broke up."

Dawson's head jerked to the side so fast, he wrenched a muscle. Bliven didn't notice, a couple of pretty Paints on the other side of a white wooden fence had caught his attention.

"The Sheriff and Sage used to go out?"

"Yeah. For quite a while. We had a pool going on when they were going to get married."

Chapter Six

TWO HOURS LATER, Dawson was cruising the SUV down Main Street, his whole body vibrating with the effort of holding in his outrage. Bliven had picked up on the tension and had hardly said a word since they'd passed the Carrigan spread.

"They make a good burger at Grey's Saloon," Bliven said. His stomach had been rumbling for the past thirty minutes.

Dawson parked, then tossed him the keys. He could tell Bliven was starting to get a little pissed off about the driving situation. He supposed he'd have to relinquish control for the afternoon. Least of his worries right now.

"Order me a burger, would you?" he said, walking in the opposite direction from his new partner. "I have a quick errand I need to handle."

That would piss off Bliven, as well, but he needed to talk to Sage. Now.

He flung open the door to Copper Mountain Chocolates, setting off a wild jangling of bells. A skinny woman who looked like she needed to eat more chocolate jumped, acting as shocked as if he'd pulled out a gun and asked her to empty the cash.

"C-can I help you?"

He gave the room a quick once-over. "Sage in the back?"

"Yes, but you can't—"

"Don't worry. We're old friends." His boots thudded loudly on the polished wood plank floors as he headed for the door. He wasn't sure what he expected to see on the other side. Maybe Sage stirring a pot of melted chocolate in a big cast iron pot?

But instead he saw a mini-factory. A counter full of equipment he didn't recognize. A large industrial sized double sink and big wooden working table holding molds of freshly made chocolates.

And it was loud.

Sage was standing with her back to him, wearing headphones and listening to music, judging by the sway of her hips. She was wearing a dress today with a pair of black flats. With her graceful height she didn't need heels to look good in a dress.

He hung back, banking his anger, not wanted to scare her and cause an accident. Watching her felt a bit voyeuristic, but damn she looked fine. If only he could put his hands on those hips and swing her around and kiss her.

She picked up a pot of melted chocolate and as he watched, she poured it over a cookie sheet covered with granola. The smell was incredible, a rich toasted scent that was sweet, spicy and rich all at the same time.

Using a rubber scraper thing she cleaned every bit of chocolate from the pot, then grabbed a fat metal knife and smoothed the chocolate until she had an even coating over the granola.

As soon as she put down the knife, he stepped to her side, where she would see him.

Her pretty eyes widened, but she didn't jump. She just calmly removed the headset, then turned off a dial on one of the machines. The room was instantly much quieter.

He didn't wait for her to ask him what he was doing there.

"Why didn't you tell me you had a thing with the Sheriff?"

"So you heard about that, did you?"

That really pushed his buttons. "You could have warned me."

She surprised him by grabbing hold of his arm and leading him toward the back exit. "Come on. I can't have you in my clean kitchen." At the door she peeled off her gloves, removed her apron, then pushed him out to the alley.

He could have resisted, easily. But it was kind of hot having her manhandle him like this.

"You knew about my new job. The least you could have done was tell me you and the Sheriff had history." It was satisfying to finally let loose some of the steam that had been mounting during the long drive back to town.

She didn't seem overly impressed. "I don't see why it would be your business. I'm not asking you for a list of the people you dated after we—split up."

He couldn't believe how cool she was being about this. "But he's old, damn it."

"Just nine years more than me."

"And he's my boss! Hell—did you tell him about me?"

"Only that I was involved with a cowboy on the circuit for a while. I never mentioned your name." She put her hands on her hips. "Does that make you feel better?"

"No, damn it. It doesn't." He'd have felt better if his name was tattooed somewhere on her body—anonymity had absolutely no appeal to him. "I can't believe you dated someone to the point where you almost got married." What would he have done if that had happened? He couldn't stand thinking about it.

"What did you figure, Dawson? That time would stand still and I'd be here in Marietta waiting for you to come and sweep me off my feet?"

He stared at her, words jammed in his throat. Yeah. He'd thought that. Jamie MacCreadie had mentioned the chocolate store. He'd never said a word about Sage dating the Sheriff.

"You know what, Dawson? This is just about as insulting as you not telling me—not once, in all those months we hung out together—that you were married."

"Hang on, I'm the one who's pissed off here."

"Only because you're deluded. What gives you the right to march into *my* store and act like I somehow *belong* to you?"

DAWSON GAVE HER a look that just about melted her heart and made her forget all the reasons she was so mad at him. His look told her he wanted to possess her all right. Here and now, in the alley if need be.

Her body, suddenly hot, screamed to be touched. Kissed. Loved.

But her mind knew better.

"I understand you're ready to settle down with your daughter, O'Dell. But maybe you should have picked another town." There was just too much history, too much banked emotion, hurt and betrayal for them to ever be the kind of ex-lovers who could just meet on the street and say 'how do you do.'

"You really mean that? You wish I'd never come back?"

She didn't want to hurt him, further. But they were both so wounded by what they had been—and what had been stripped away from them. So she nodded.

His green eyes narrowed just the tiniest amount. "Fine." He punched out the word. Gritted his teeth. Started to leave, then turned back. "I'll keep my distance if that's what you want. But as for me packing my bags and moving to a different town… It's not happening, I decided to make a new life here for my daughter, and that's what I'm going to do."

Her mouth grew dry as she listened to him. He started to leave, walking in that long-strided athletic way of his. But then he stopped and took the same number of steps back to her.

"Just so you know what you're missing." And then he reached for her, pulling her close, putting a hand under her chin and kissing her in a very rough and meaningful way.

She didn't push away, she was too breathless, too swept up into the moment.

Her knees went weak and she grabbed onto him, feeling his powerful arms, the muscles bunched up and hard.

She knew his taste, the brush of his skin, the shape of his lips.

Something primitive inside her said, *mine.*

And then he was stepping back and in a husky voice he asked. "The Sheriff. Do you still love him?"

Her head was spinning. First the kiss. Then that question. As a matter of principle, she shouldn't even answer. But if she'd meant what she'd told him—that he should leave her alone, then maybe this was the way to make it happen.

"I don't know. It wasn't that long ago that we split up. He asked me to think about marrying him." None of those statements were lies. The only lie was giving the impression that she *was* thinking about the offer, that she *hadn't* given a definitive no.

But her answer did the trick. His entire face tightened and a layer of frost seemed to go up over his mossy green eyes. “Thanks for telling me that,” his said quietly. “I’m glad you were honest.”

And then he was gone, and she knew he meant it, that he wasn’t going to bother her anymore. The kiss had been his way of reminding her what they had been. And could never be again. Especially not now that she’d put up that barrier between them.

She stayed where she was, watching as he reached the end of alley then turned right toward Main Street. True to his word, he never even looked back.

BACK IN THE kitchen she washed up at the sink, inhaling deeply and trying to calm herself.

It was only a kiss. She would be okay. She was strong enough to handle anything.

Dakota opened the door, and without stepping over the threshold, asked breathlessly. “Is he gone?”

“Yup.” And for good this time. It was what she’d wanted and what she’d asked for, but it still made her feel unbearably empty inside.

“Was that Dawson O’Dell? Craig and I saw him at the rodeo this weekend. He was amazing. And so cute. If he’s a friend of yours, you should ask him if he would model for your next advertisement. A few pictures of him around here would sure bring in the business."

"We're selling chocolate, not western wear."

"Sex sells anything," Dakota insisted. "Especially chocolate."

AT THE END of his shift, Dawson went back to the motel to change out of his uniform. The afternoon had seemed to drag on forever, Bliven's good mood had returned after he'd eaten his burger. Dawson hadn't been able to stomach more than a few mouthfuls of his.

All his plans, everything he'd dreamed of for the past five years, had just gone south.

He supposed he'd been a fool to shoot for the stars. But he was back to earth now. Why would Sage be interested in a first-year deputy when she had the Sheriff of the town asking her to marry him. Hell, he'd grown up in a series of townhouses and condos. While her family owned one of the biggest ranches in Park County.

He was a boy who'd grown up with a footloose and fancy free mother and six fathers, who in sum total had meant less to him than his favorite horse. She came from a real family, with land, a heritage, and values he hadn't had much exposure to in his life.

Most guys would laugh if he told them what had attracted him to her in the first place. It wasn't her lean, sexy body, or undeniably pretty face. It wasn't the way she moved when she was on her horse, or that long red braid she wore tossed over one shoulder.

There was something wholesome about her, that set her off from the rest.

And he'd been drawn to that.

The more he got to know her, the more he'd seen that her goodness, her stability and her values, weren't just icing on some cake—they ran right through her.

At the time, he'd believed he could change. For the past five years he'd hung on to that dream.

But deep down he was still the same guy. A guy who had grown up never really belonging anywhere. Or with anyone. He'd spent too many evenings drinking too much, and bedding too many women. Hell, he'd been the kind of idiot who would decide to marry on a whim, and then get that woman pregnant when he had no intention of staying with her.

Dawson put on his jeans and an old gray T-shirt that had seen too many washings. He had plans to meet his mother and Savannah for dinner at the diner in ten minutes. When he'd made the suggestion earlier, his mother had given him her long-suffering look. He suspected she was getting weary of the home-style cooking places he favored.

Which was good. Hopefully she'd get so sick of the food she'd head back to Florida and her nice condo on the golf course. She'd been traveling with him and Savannah for about a month now and his patience was getting thin.

When he stepped into the familiar eatery, exactly on time, he had to look a few times to make sure his mother had brought Savannah with her.

He bit back a curse when he realized she had.

His daughter was pimped up like one of those poor children on that Tots with Tiaras show. Her hair had been curled and styled, she was wearing a shiny pink dress and—holy crap—his mother had even put makeup on her.

He wanted to grab his little girl and throw her in the nearest shower.

But he wasn't such a fool that he didn't realize he might hurt Savannah's feelings badly by doing that. So he forced a smile and took a seat. "Hi, there. Hope everyone is hungry. Connie cooks turkey pot pie on Mondays and boy is it good."

"Did you give any tickets at your job today, Daddy?"

"Not yet." Although he was avoiding looking at her directly, he could see his mother was nursing a glass of white wine and wincing each time she took a swallow. He guessed the house Sauvignon Blanc wasn't up to her standards.

"Doesn't Savannah look pretty today?" Patricia finally had to force the issue.

"She always looks pretty to me."

"Do you like my dress, Daddy? And my hair? Grandma bought me nice things for a treat."

"It's really fancy, that's for sure. And it's fun to place

dress up now and then. But I hope your grandma also bought you some jeans and T-shirts? Because that's the sort of stuff you'll need to wear to school." He fired a glance at his mother then, hoping she registered the depth of his anger.

His daughter was not a doll, for God's sake.

When they finished their meal, Savannah asked if they could go to the park.

He shook his head.

"But I want to play on the monkey bars," Savannah protested. "And fly on the swings. I never got to have any fun today. Me and Grandma were shopping all the time."

"You can't go to the park in a fancy dress like that. Once you've changed, I'll take you out to play. Wait here at the table, while Grandma and I go to pay the bill."

He waited until his mother reluctantly left her seat, then took her to the hallway that led to the washrooms where he could still see his daughter, but she couldn't overhear the conversation.

"What the hell, Mom?"

She glared at him. "Why are you being so rude?"

"You really expected thanks? How could you do that to her? She's only five years old! What kind of message do you think you're giving her?"

His mother had a cold look in her eyes that he remembered all too well, having been on the receiving end of it a lot in his youth. "I had hoped that you would be a little more appreciative of all I've done to help you and Savannah since Gina left."

"This time. Since Gina left *this time,*" he corrected. "Gina is always coming and going. It doesn't change anything. I take care of my kid and when I have to work, I hire sitters."

Okay. That had come out a little too brutal. Dawson took a breath. "You have been great, Mom. And I do want you to be part of Savannah's life. But if you're honest you have to admit you don't really want to live here. There aren't enough shopping malls, or golf courses, or nice restaurants."

"You make me sound so shallow."

"I didn't mean that as criticism. Lots of people prefer living in Florida to life in a small Montana town. But not me. This place feels right to me, and I'm going to settle in and make a real home for my daughter."

Her eyelids fluttered. "But you'll have shift work. And what happens when you're on nights?"

"I'll hire sitters, just the way I did when I needed to work at the rodeo. I've already got a day home lined up and several women with references for the after-hours stuff. We're going to be fine."

His mother's face suddenly looked caved in to him. Wrinkled and old, despite her make-up and artificially blonde hair.

"I was a good mother to you, wasn't I, honey? You always had clean clothes and plenty of food to eat. I was nice to you, never yelled or hit you…"

No. But the men she married had. They'd moved homes almost once a year, and she'd never encouraged him at school, always saying a pass was good enough.

But she'd given birth to him and raised him and he really did believe she'd done the best that she was capable of.

"You were a good mother. And you're a good grandmother, too. I just think Savannah and I are ready to be on our own."

CALLAN TEXTED SAGE at nine o'clock on Saturday night. "At Grey's. Come have a drink."

Sage had already changed into her flannel PJs. By mid-October the nights were getting cooler. She'd just selected a movie on Netflix and made popcorn. It had been a long week.

"Tired," she texted back.

"Need help. Cowboys buying me too many drinks."

Sage laughed, then swore. It was so not true. If anyone needed rescuing it was the cowboys, not her tough younger sister. Yet, Callan had played to her weakness, knowing that Sage worried about her drinking and wouldn't be able to resist coming to check on her.

As Sage switched out her comfy flannels for a denim dress and the red boots Dani had talked her into buying on their last trip to Missoula, she tried to tell herself she was being overprotective. Callan worked hard all week and deserved to have fun on the weekend.

But it still didn't seem right that for Callan, fun always involved too many beers and the wrong kind of men. As far as Sage knew, the good times usually ended at the swinging doors that led from the saloon to the street. Too smart to drive, Callan would walk all the way to Sage's place and decamp on the sofa.

Sage took her bike, as usual, cycling carefully so she wouldn't catch her skirt in the chain. At Grey's she locked up, feeling like an old time cowgirl hitching her horse to a post outside the saloon.

Inside, the party had definitely started without her. She was recognized by a group of friends she'd hung out with in high school and stopped to chat.

"You should have seen Chelsea in here last weekend," one of the guys told her. "Boy did that girl let her hair down for the rodeo."

"It wasn't for the rodeo, you idiot. It was for that rich guy from California. The one who's turning the old railway depot into a microbrewery," his date corrected him.

"Right. Jasper Flint," Dean continued. "Have you seen his motorbike? That thing is bloody beautiful."

"They're quite the item, I hear."

"Flint and his bike?"

"No." The date was exasperated. "Flint and *Chelsea.*"

This exchange had Sage baffled. Chelsea was letting her hair down for Jasper Flint, the rich playboy oil tycoon from

California? Impossible. But just then she noticed her sister, sitting at the long, wide bar. "I've got to go meet Callan. Catch you later."

Weaving between tables, she was making progress on reaching her goal, when a new angle allowed her to see the cowboy sitting next to Callan.

Dawson.

Sage stopped dead. Would she ever be able to see him without feeling her heart slam up against her chest? He'd better not be the one plying her sister with drinks and hitting on her. But his body language wasn't offensive. He had both hands on his bottle of beer and his broad shoulders were hunched, as if he was nursing something more than the beverage. Something like a heartache?

Sage was already backing up, thinking this was a scene she ought to avoid. But then Callan flung her hair over her shoulder and spotted her.

"Hey, sis, come on over."

Dawson stumbled to his feet. "You're sisters?" He glanced from one to the other. "Ah—Cal is Callan. I should have figured. You have similar smiles."

"Hang on. You guys know each other? Sit down Dawson. I need details." Callan was dressed in tight jeans and a low cut tank top, a look she could get away with given her small, athletic figure. "Jason, we need another round here."

Callan was one of few people who dared snap her fingers at gruff old Jason Grey. Jason was old school when it came to bar tending. He wasn't here to be anyone's friend or sounding board. He served drinks—and if he didn't like you, those drinks might be a long time coming.

Sage had always been a little afraid of him. "I'll have whatever my sister's drinking, please." She sat on Callan's right-hand side, leaning forward so she could see Dawson. "And how did you two meet?"

"I spotted Mr. All-Around about half an hour ago and insisted he buy me a drink. He was kind enough to oblige. Before you challenge him to a duel or something, he's been a perfect gentleman."

Sage was concerned when she heard the slurring between Callan's words. "Dawson and I know each other from the rodeo circuit. Where's your daughter?" she asked pointedly.

"With her grandma," Callan was the one to answer, proving that she and Dawson had already covered a lot of ground in their conversation.

"It's Mom's last weekend in Marietta and she wanted to spend the evening with her granddaughter. Though, hopefully Savannah is sleeping by now."

He sounded like any concerned parent.

She wasn't used to him in that role. But it suited him.

"I was tellin' Dawson about the round-up next Friday. Dad's got a crew of eight lined up, counting me and Sage." Callan nodded her head in Dawson's direction. "He's a top ranking cowboy and he's never been on one. Can you believe it?"

Sage could. She knew Dawson and his mother had lived primarily in cities, except for the two years Patricia had been married to her fourth husband. She'd met him—Earl, Sage thought it was—while gambling in Nevada. Earl had some land and horses, and he'd been the one to introduce Dawson to riding.

He'd been immediately hooked and had started saving his money to go to every rodeo clinic within driving distance. By the time his mother and Earl had split up, Dawson was on his own, working behind the scenes at the rodeo until he was old enough to sign up with the CPRA.

Sage took a drink of the beer Jason had just set in front of her. "Dawson has a job. And a daughter. I doubt he could make it."

"Well, duh, he should bring his kid. It's a family event, right? We've got several cooks lined up to help with the big barbecue afterward and they'll all be bringing their children, too. Your daughter will have a hoot playing while you live out your deepest cowboy fantasies." Callan glanced from Dawson to Sage. "The non-X-rated ones, I mean."

"It's a nice offer, but I don't want to butt in on a family affair."

Dawson was saying the right words, but Sage could see the yearning in his eyes. He would so love to do this. And now that they'd finally put closure to their relationship, wasn't it kind of mean of her not to let him?

"No, really, Callan's right. You should come. It'll be

amazing."

"You're sure?"

She wasn't. But she nodded anyway. Shortly after that, Dawson made an excuse to leave, cleared their tab, then said good-bye.

Sage stared at the bottle on the bar, rather than watch him leave. Her chest ached with sadness remembering the way he'd looked at her. Distant. Sad. This was what she'd asked for, and yet it felt terrible.

Callan bumped her shoulder. "Do you want to tell me what's up with you two?"

"Nope."

"I didn't think so."

Chapter Seven

IT WAS A funny thing. Now that Dawson had backed off and agreed to leave her alone, Sage wasn't nearly as mad at him anymore. It was actually kind of frustrating. Because that kiss he'd left her with had been off the charts and not so easy to forget.

That was why he'd done it of course. So he could drive her crazy with wanting him.

And then he'd chatted up her sister at the bar the other night, in another one of his devious plans…

But no. Sage didn't really believe that.

He was being true to his word and leaving her alone. And it had been Callan who'd cornered him at the bar, not the other way around. She had that straight from sister's mouth.

No, this wasn't another stage in his strategy to win her over.

He'd truly given up. And she ought to be glad but she wasn't.

About an hour after opening her shop on Monday morning, Sage was surprised by a visit from Dawson's mother. Patricia was in tapered slacks and a button-up cardigan. Large sunglasses were perched on her head and she carried a clutch the same deep red color as her sweater.

"I've got a flight out of Bozeman this afternoon. Thought I'd pick up something sweet to take home with me."

Tall and thin, Patricia looked like the kind of woman who ate salads and drank sparkling water—not one who purchased a box of chocolates for no special reason. Suspecting Dawson's mother had something else on her agenda, Sage pointed out some of her customers' favorites, then invited her to browse.

Patricia grabbed the closest box and took it to the cash.

"So, do you miss the rodeo life, Sage?"

Her smooth, pseudo-friendly voice had Sage immediately on guard. "Not at all."

Sage could sense the older woman sizing her up, but she kept focused on completing the transaction, punching in the numbers, then handing the credit machine over so Patricia could insert her card.

"Ever since Dawson told me that he was moving here, I've been trying to figure out why. Marietta's a nice enough place, but, well, frankly it's small and in the middle of nowhere."

Which was exactly why people liked it so much. But no point telling Patricia that. She wouldn't get it.

"But when I met you," Patricia continued, "I finally worked it out."

Sage packaged the chocolates, slipped in the receipt. "I don't get the connection, Mrs. O'Dell."

"Anderson." A note of annoyance crept into her voice. "My last name is Anderson. And of course you must realize that Dawson moved here because of you. The real reason I stopped in today—"

Ah…here it comes. Sage kept a blank expression on her face as she waited.

"—is to warn you. Dawson may think Marietta is the perfect place to raise a child. But I know my son. And he's going to get bored here. Fast."

It was possible she was right, Sage had to concede. But why would any mother feel compelled to warn a perfect stranger—because that's what the two of them were—at the risk of hurting her own son?

Patricia *wanted* Dawson to be unhappy here. She *wanted* him to move. Her son was making choices that suggested Patricia's own choices had been wrong.

And she couldn't deal with that.

"You're sweet to be concerned," she said. "But I'm sure everything will work out the way it's meant to."

Patricia looked puzzled. Clearly her warning hadn't engendered the response she'd been hoping for.

"Have a safe trip home," Sage continued, her words a dismissal as she moved to help a middle-aged couple who'd just entered the store.

BUSINESS THAT WEEK picked up as the days rolled by, but for Sage there was less satisfaction than usual in making and selling her own special confections. Even the autumn colors seemed less beautiful than before.

She thought about Dawson more than she should, and found herself looking forward to the round-up when she would be seeing him again.

True to his word, he didn't "bother her" before that.

On Thursday night, she closed up the shop as usual, then rode her bike by Rose's house to leave her the key. By special arrangement Rose and Dakota would be manning the store without her tomorrow.

With that job done, Sage cycled home, packed her overnight bag, then headed to the ranch for the night. They'd be getting up before dawn tomorrow and she wanted every extra minute of sleep that she could muster.

SAGE'S FATHER AND Callan had just finished dinner when Sage arrived at the Circle C. First thing she noticed was how tired Hawksley looked. Callan was right. He was getting too old to work as hard as when he was younger.

She set a box of chocolate-covered gingers on the table, the kind her father loved, though he'd never admit it.

"Sorry we didn't wait for you," Callan said. "But there's plenty of chili left in the pot. And corn bread and salad."

Sage glanced at the big, gas stove. There were two pots—one with beef chili and the other vegetarian. She got out a bowl and tried a little of each. Settling down at her usual spot she asked, "Is everything set for tomorrow?"

Callan chatted away, while Hawksley took a few candies, then set off for the adjoining family room and his favorite recliner. When Sage was done with the chili, she had some salad then helped her sister clean the kitchen.

When they were finished, she told Callan she'd take their father his cup of tea. She found her dad snoozing in front of a blaring television. When she switched it off, his eyes popped open.

She set the mug on the table next to his chair, then made herself comfy on the sofa.

"Eliza Bramble invited me for coffee this week."

Up went her father's eyebrows, but he kept staring at the screen even though it was now blank.

"She's writing a book about her family's history."

Her father's lips curled. "What's she calling it? The Almighty Brambles of Marietta, Montana? Bet it'll be a real bestseller."

Her father's disdain for the family that had refused to welcome him to their fold wasn't news to Sage.

"I know. But I suppose it's something for Eliza to do. Must be pretty boring running a small town bed and breakfast when she's used to working for a big company."

"Oh, she's keeping busy all right. Making sure she gets what she wants from crazy old Mabel."

"Do you really think Mabel has a lot of money? The house is looking run-down if you ask me."

"That's what they want us to think," Hawksley insisted. "Not that I care. The Brambles never impressed me a bit and I sure as hell never needed their money."

Sage had known this wouldn't be easy. "Well, anyway, it can't hurt to help Eliza with her research. She was just wondering if Mom had any old letters or—"

She got no further. Hawksley grabbed the armrests of his chair and pulled his body forward. "Stop right there. Nothing of your mother's is leaving this house."

After their mother's death, Sage remembered her father going through Beverly's closet, boxing clothing and personal effects. He'd done this when she and her sisters were supposed to be sleeping, but they had known what was going on.

After, all that had been left was a bunch of cardboard boxes with their Mom's name that their father kept at the back of the closet. Each of them had been given a box when they turned eighteen. Sage's had contained a pearl necklace that her mother had been given by her parents, a book of poetry her mother had loved, and a handful of photos, mostly of her and her mother together.

She'd been touched at how carefully her father had made

his selections, ensuring each of his daughters had something precious and meaningful to remember their mother by.

But there were still a couple of those boxes left in the closet—and she didn't think any of her sisters had ever dared pry apart the packing tape to peer inside. "But, Dad. Couldn't I just look—"

"Absolutely not, Sage. You got that?"

THE SUN HADN'T yet risen when Dawson pulled up to the Carrigan's ranch house ten days after he'd scored the invitation from Callan—with Sage's blessing, or he never would have come. Savannah woke up when the truck stopped. With their lifestyle she was used to hitting the road early. She was also good at meeting new people, it was something she had to do every time they pulled in to the next rodeo, so she didn't make shy at all about going into this strange house to meet a whole new gang of folks.

He wished he could say the same.

The prospect of meeting Sage's father had him a little trepidatious. In Sage's stories he was always larger than life—a man who was almost impossible to please. Would Dawson stick out like the greenhorn he was? He was determined not to. His cowboy pride was on the line.

A stream of people were coming and going from a side entrance to the house. They smiled with mild curiosity, but no one stopped to chat. Everyone had a job to do—the goal being to be in the saddle when the sun broke over the horizon.

Turned out the side entrance led to a mud room, then through to the biggest kitchen he'd ever seen. There were five woman of various ages bustling around preparing sandwiches, and wrapping cookies and fruit for the cowboys to pack in their saddle bags. But they all paused in their work to say hi to Savannah. And his little girl won their hearts right after they invited her to join the other kids, sprawled on the comfy sofas in the attached family room, sleepily watching cartoons.

"Thank-you," Savannah said politely. "I'll do that. But if you need any help, let me know. I'm real good at making sandwiches."

"You done good raising her," one of the women told him when Savannah left the room. She looked to be in her late forties, a stocky woman with a square jaw and kind brown eyes.

He introduced himself and asked for her name.

"I'm Emma Flanagan—I'm the one in charge of this crew."

"You sure it's okay I leave Savannah in your care?"

"We'll all keep an eye on her," Emma promised.

"Been doing this all our lives and haven't lost a kid yet," joked another one of the women.

He gave her a stern look, not appreciating the humor. She just laughed at him. "She's in good hands, cowboy. Go out and enjoy your day."

IN FRONT OF the stable, Dawson found the horses saddled and ready to go. Hawksley was already mounted on a big black gelding, perched like a king on his throne, watching the proceedings impatiently. Dawson waited for the man's gaze to settle on him, before introducing himself.

"Dawson O'Dell, sir. Met your daughter Callan the other day." Smarter, maybe, not to mention where. "She said you could use an extra hand."

"Callan, huh? I thought you were the cowboy who came round the hospital the day after Sage injured her knee."

How had he known that? "That's me, too."

Hawksley let out an unimpressed hrumph, then indicated a dappled gray, about a hand smaller than his own mount. "You can ride old Pinstripes here. Hopefully you'll stick better today than you did at the rodeo on Saturday."

His score that afternoon hadn't been so bad that it prevented him from winning the big purse, but Dawson didn't bother mentioning this. You proved yourself to men like Hawksley by working hard, being competent, and not talking too much.

He took a few minutes to acquaint himself with Pinstripes. Rubbing the spots under his eyes and scratching his withers, he spoke to the horse in a low, calm voice.

"We're going to have us a good day, Pinstripes. Okay

boy?"

The pattern of gray over the gelding's white coat did kind of look like pinstripes in places. A boot in the stirrup, and then he was over, and seated. Pinstripes took a few steps back, then settled nicely. The air was still cool, most of the men were wearing jackets, or down vests over their shirts.

One of the men let out a low whistle and Dawson nudged Pinstripes over, so he could see what all the men were now staring at.

Sage and Callan were riding up from the other side of the barn, Sage on a bay filly with a copper coat, black markings and a chiseled face. They were an astonishingly pretty pair and his heart soared to see her on a horse again. Much as she'd hated the competitors' ring, he could see why her father had pushed her into her rodeo career. She was such a damn natural.

With all the riders present, Hawksley started pairing them up. Dawson looked for Callan, certain that Sage wouldn't want to ride with him. But she surprised him by coming up on his left and calling to her father, "I'll ride with the new guy."

Hawksley frowned, but didn't waste time disagreeing. A band of orange and gold light was cresting the hills to the east. It was time to go.

At first all eight of them rode abreast. It must have been quite a sight but Dawson didn't need a photograph. He knew he'd remember this all his life. Sage must have caught him grinning, because she smiled back.

"Nothing quite like it, is there?"

He rode horses almost every day, but this was a reminder of where it had all started and what it was about. Survival in the West had depended on these sorts of skills. Moving the cattle up to the high hills in the spring and summer. Then bringing them back home before the howling winds and snow of winter.

They crossed over a bridge and then through a gate. Now the riders were spreading out, but he noticed Sage still kept close to him. The sun was definitely over the mountains now, making the new snow on the peaks sparkle. The same light grazed over the trees down on the slopes, picking out the golden leaves of the cottonwoods and the reds in the lower growing shrubs. Dawson felt his throat thicken, it was all so damn beautiful. And the air. There was a special pine spice here in the valley that made his lungs feel clean and pure.

As they entered the upper range, Hawksley used hand gestures to break them into two parties. The concept was simple enough. One group would move to the left, the other to the right, working the perimeter and pushing the cows in, then meeting at the end and driving the herd forward and down to closer pastures.

"Search every coulee and thicket of woods," Hawksley hollered out. "It's easier to find the cows the first time then go back for them later."

After that, the distances between the riders widened further, but Sage pulled her mount up beside his.

"We'll head this way," Sage pointed left. "I know a few favorite hiding places that Dad wants me to check."

Rather than ride single-file, though, she kept her filly abreast of his.

"Thanks for letting me experience this."

"Figured it was about time you put those riding skills of your to some practical use."

"You sound just like your father when you say that."

She laughed. "Oh my God. Don't tell Callan."

Twenty minutes went by of very comfortable silence. The more they pushed forward, the more Dawson felt as if they were sliding back in time, falling into the rhythm of being together in a nice and natural way.

Sage pointed out the lee side of a grassy hill. "Mattie and I saw a black bear there once. Didn't even notice us, thank goodness."

"See a lot of bear?" He couldn't help looking over both shoulders.

"We know they're here. But we rarely actually see one. When we do, it makes for a good story."

A few minutes later, he was the first to speak. "So why the chocolate shop? I never remember you saying you'd like to do something like that."

"That was a twist of fate for sure. When my knee was still in a brace, Dani took me on a trip to New York City to cheer me up."

He felt a twinge of guilt, suspecting he—and not her injured knee—was the reason she'd been depressed in the first place.

"We happened to walk into a specialty chocolate store that was doing tastings of single-origin beans."

"Huh?"

"In some ways making chocolate is like producing wine. You can blend different varieties of grapes the way chocolatiers blend cacao beans from different varieties of cacao trees. But a purist will prefer a single varietal like a Shiraz, over a blend.

"That's impressive." Seeing her kitchen and the photos in her store, he already knew her business was a lot more complicated than it seemed from the outside.

"I wish my father thought so. He thinks I'm a chicken for giving up after just one injury." She put a hand on her knee. "Maybe I am."

"Bull."

She twisted around in the saddle to check out his expression. "Why do you say that?"

"When you wake up every day for four years and do something that scares you to death?" Which is what she'd done during her career as a barrel-racer. "That's called courage in my books."

DAWSON COULDN'T HAVE said anything nicer to her, Sage thought, mulling over his words as they continued to ride. She'd carried the burden of being a coward for a long time. But what he said, did make sense. And it was nice to know that he saw her, not as week and afraid, but strong and brave.

A minute later she spotted the first of the cows, two black baldies and their calves grazing in a green pocket behind some white pine. She pointed them out to Dawson so he could do the work of flushing them out. Her father had been smart to pair him with old Pinstripes. The dappled gray knew exactly what to do, and Dawson returned from the task with his eyes bright. "Damn, this is fun."

They were too busy to do much talking after that.

About six hours later, they met the rest of the riders at the back of the range. They had the beginnings of their herd now and it was time to push forward.

"Where's your All-Around Cowboy, Sage?" her father asked.

Sage hadn't realized she'd lost him. She looked at the trail behind her but didn't see any sign of Dawson.

"Time's a-wasting, girl. He better not be taking photographs or some foolish—"

He stopped talking then as Dawson emerged from a scrub of pines, pushing a bawling heifer calf toward the herd. Almost immediately the mother separated herself from the others and came to greet her.

Sage smiled. *Well done, Dawson.* But of course her father

gave no praise, just nodded, and got on with the business of moving the cattle.

By the time they made it back to the ranch it was almost seven and the light was getting thin. Sage felt bone weary as she filled the grain bags for Cinnamon Girl and Pinstripes. While she was doing that, Dawson lifted off the saddle for her and took it to the tack room. He came back, impressed.

"This is quite the outfit, your family ranch. Some of those saddles are valuable antiques. I bet they're worth as much as a small car."

"And they get great mileage, too, since they run on a little hay and some oats."

He pushed her shoulder playfully, then they walked together to the side door. They had to wait in line for a chance to wash up in the mudroom, and the good smells coming from the kitchen had her stomach rumbling.

"Hi, Daddy. Hi Sage." Savannah was there to greet them, looking perfectly content and holding a picture she'd colored for her father. While he admired the drawing of horses and mountains, she kept chatting. "I made some friends and helped the ladies in the kitchen. Did you move the cows?"

"We sure did. It was a lot of fun." He smiled at Sage, before letting his daughter lead him to the buffet table where a full roast beef dinner was waiting for them. Not just succulent sliced beef, but also gravy and horseradish, mashed potatoes and carrots and turnips. And a big salad, which most of the cowboys didn't touch.

Sage checked in with Callan to see how she was faring. "You're used to this," she said. "My legs and butt are going to be killing me tomorrow."

"What can I say, you're getting soft." Callan helped herself to loads of the vegetables and the salad. It was an unspoken understanding among all the sisters that she was a vegetarian, but the unspoken part was key because if she dared say such a thing aloud their father would surely have a heart attack.

"So your cowboy did good today," Callan said when they had found a seat around the spacious dining room table.

"Not mine."

"Could have fooled me. You stuck pretty close to him today."

"Just didn't want him getting into Dad's crosshairs." Which was kind of ironic, when she thought about it.

"Isn't that sweet. But I have a feeling Dawson will have no trouble handling our father."

After Sage had finished her second helping, plus a slice of chokecherry pie, Savannah suddenly appeared in front of her. "We have to go home now. Daddy says I should say thank you, even though it was the other ladies who watched over me and made me my meals."

"You're right. I didn't do much, did I?"

"You helped move the cows," Savannah said, defending her. "Your hair is pretty. Does it grow that color or do you have to go to the shop like my grandma?"

"It grows this way."

"Stop chattering, Savannah, it's time to go home." Dawson came round the corner then, scooping up his daughter.

Savannah laughed, then snuggled into his shoulder.

"You must be tired. It's been a long day," he said.

Sage walked out to the driveway with them. Watched as Dawson snapped Savannah into her seat, then planted a kiss on her head. For a rough-and-ready cowboy he was proving to be an amazing dad. But the tenderness in his expression vanished when he turned to face Sage.

All signs of the easy friendship they'd settled into today were gone.

"It was a great day, Sage. I half expected to see my boss out here, though."

She glanced away, unwilling to admit that she'd used her ex-boyfriend as a ruse. She still didn't know why she'd done it. If today had proven anything, it was that she still loved Dawson.

She knew he felt the same way.

Yet, how did you go about trusting someone who had let you down so badly?

"Don't worry," Dawson said. "I understand this day doesn't change anything between us."

And then he left. And she stood there, heart aching with the burden of all the unsaid words between them.

INSTEAD OF GOING back to the house, which was still full of cowboys and their families, Sage headed for the horse barn, calling out for her father, then finding him in the tack room, oiling one of his favorite saddles.

He'd never been comfortable in large, social settings. But she wished he would at least sit down to rest. "Aren't you tired, Dad?"

"It was a big day. Got me thinking about my old man and all the times we worked together moving cattle."

The saddle, she realized then, was the practically antique one that had belonged to her grandfather. Her father didn't often talk about his past. But she knew he'd adored his father. Maybe that was why he'd been so set on having a son—so he could have a similar relationship with one of his own children.

It hurt to know that he didn't consider any of his daughters worthy of the effort.

But that was an old sorrow. One Sage hoped she had come to terms with.

"Dad, if you knew Mom was having an affair, why didn't you ask her to leave?"

He winced. "Does this have something to do with that damn history of the Brambles?"

"No. You don't want to help Eliza and I get that."

"Then why bring your mother up now?"

"You think there'll ever be a better time?"

He gave one of his characteristic rough hrumphs.

"So why didn't you, Dad? Ask her to leave?"

"It's not that simple."

"But—" Actually it seemed that way to her. "It was a pretty big betrayal."

"There are worse, believe it or not." He straightened, putting a hand to his lower back.

She took the rag from him, added a bit of oil, and started working on the old leather. "I'm not sure what could be worse."

Her dad perched on one of the sawhorses, settling his weight with a heavy sigh. "Did you stop to think what Bill was talking about the other night when he said I had a lot to answer for?"

"I didn't think he meant much by it."

"Well, he did. When your mother was young, she had a lot of fellows trying to court her—Bill and me included. She was a real beauty, and boy could she dance. For some reason she picked me, but I guess she soon regretted that. She was a town girl, had no clue about ranch living. I figured she'd adjust, but she didn't. I think she was awful unhappy out here, Sage. And to be perfectly honest, there were times I wish I'd married a more ordinary woman."

He was telling her that her parents' marriage hadn't been perfect. But lots of marriages weren't. "It was her choice to marry you."

"Yup. And she lived with the consequences."

"But the affair…"

"Another choice. And more consequences. You want to know what troubles me more than that? Knowing your mother was scared to death when she was out in that barn helping me pull that calf out of that cow. I should have made her leave, but I didn't. Yet another choice. And look where that one led."

His face was gray now, his shoulders more stooped than they'd seemed fifteen minutes ago. Sage stopped buffing the leather and went to join him on his perch. "It was an accident. Not your fault."

"That's taking the easy way out. I made a bad call. It happens. People aren't perfect. You should realize this at your age." He rubbed a hand over his forehead. "I take it Mr. All-around is the reason you're asking all these questions."

She stared down at the tips of her worn riding boots. She'd never told her father that Dawson was married. But clearly he'd picked up on the tension between them. "Maybe."

He sighed. "First time I saw him, at that hospital in Wyoming, I figured he was bad news."

"You saw him at the hospital?"

"You were already in the truck. I'd gone back to sign some papers. I heard him at the front desk asking for you."

"And you didn't tell me?"

"Like I said, he looked like bad news. However," her father added slowly. "After seeing him at the round-up today, I do believe I've changed my mind."

Chapter Eight

ON SATURDAY IT occurred to Sage that with all the drama of Dawson coming back to town, she hadn't checked in with Jenny or Chelsea for a really long time. What kind of friend was she? Poor Jenny was probably still all choked up about the aborted wedding.

As for Chelsea—was it really possible she was in the midst of a hot and heavy affair with that rich, bad-boy, oil magnate from California?

Sage sent them both text messages to see if they were free for the evening. They hadn't had a girls' night out in a while.

Jenny was the first to answer, with just a brief "busy." What the heck was that about?

Next to report in was Chelsea. "Have a hot date, but I'm two blocks away. Will stop in to say hi."

"Great," Sage texted back. Hot date, huh? Seemed like the rumors were actually well founded. She sighed, not sure if she should be concerned… or jealous. She watched out the window until she caught sight of Chelsea, long blonde hair swinging freely, dressed in a flirty skirt that was much shorter than her usual style.

The man beside her was hard-core handsome. He bent to give Chelsea the kind of kiss that didn't belong on Main Street, Marietta, then disappeared down the block. Chelsea opened the door, and stepped inside, still looking like a woman who'd been thoroughly kissed.

"I can't believe it. So the talk around town is true?"

Chelsea's flush deepened. "I can't seem to stop myself. Sometimes I feel like I'm making the biggest mistake of my life. But I've never felt so happy. Or alive."

Sage smiled, happy for her friend, but a little worried too. "That's Jasper Flint, right? Is he in town for long?"

"Yes. As in permanently."

"Really?" Sage didn't want to be skeptical. But—"The guy has a reputation on a national scale."

"Jasper has found his home here. He really has."

"So you think it's possible for people to change?"

"I think it's possible for them to *grow.*"

Interesting perspective. "Well, I'm glad for you Chels. You look amazing. Have you talked to Jenn lately? I haven't had a good talk with her since her wedding fell apart."

"She won't admit it, but she's been spending a lot of time with Colton Thorpe."

"No." Had her best friends both come down with rodeo fever this year? First Chelsea and Jasper Flint. Now Jenny and the rodeo guest chair? "I saw him in the bull riding event. My sisters were drooling over him."

"He's hot, all right. But unlike Jasper, he doesn't live in Montana anymore and he's real clear he has no plans on moving back."

"I hope Jenny isn't setting herself up for more heartache." Sage thought about that brief text message. "Busy." Now she knew doing what.

Chelsea picked out a box of caramels. "While I'm here I might as well indulge Jasper's sweet tooth." She leaned over the counter as Sage quickly processed the transaction. "And how about you? Anything new?"

Sage felt bowed by the pressure of all she was holding back in her heart. She longed to confide the entire story to her friend.

How five years ago a cowboy had stolen her heart before she realized he was married. She'd tried to forget him—but he was back. And he'd changed and matured. As Chelsea would say, he'd *grown.*

But she'd pushed him away, even though she still loved him.

And now she was afraid that she'd hurt him too much for him to give her a second chance. All from a flash of ugly anger. A desire to hurt him the way he'd hurt her.

"I spent most of my weekend either working or with my family. Matt and Dani were in town for the weekend."

"Nice. Sorry I missed them." Chelsea picked up her chocolates. "I'd better run. We'll get together soon, okay?"

"Sounds good."

Once Chelsea was gone—back to the lover who was undoubtedly more delicious than the chocolates she'd just purchased for him—Sage felt more alone than ever. Callan and her father were busy separating this year's weanlings for market. And Dani was away on a conference in Australia.

At lunch time, hoping she would catch Mattie in the house, rather than outside working with the horses, Sage placed a call to her oldest sister.

Mattie answered after the first ring, as if she'd been hovering over the phone. "Is everything okay? I don't usually hear from you in the middle of the day."

"We're all fine," Sage reassured her. "I just thought I'd mention something interesting that happened last week. Eliza Bramble invited me in for coffee. Turns out she's writing a book about the Bramble family history and she's hoping for access to Mom's old papers, letters, that sort of thing."

"Maybe there's some in those boxes in his closet?"

"Yeah, I thought of those, too. But when I asked dad if we could check them out, he shut me right down."

"Well, you know how he hates that side of the family."

"I do." Sage hesitated. "Did you and Dani ever sneak a look in those boxes?"

"When Mom was still alive we used to go play with her make-up and jewelry—remember?"

"Oh, I sure do." Though she'd never done it again since that last, awful time.

"But after she died, Dad threw out the make-up and gave away her clothes. I never felt right going in their room again. I'm pretty sure Dani was the same."

"So we have no idea what's in those remaining boxes. I just got the impression from Great Aunt Mable and Eliza that they think Mom might have had something important hidden away. Could there be some big family secret we don't know about?"

"Like what?" Mattie laughed. "Just tell Eliza we don't have anything left of Mom's and leave it at that.

"I will," Sage agreed. What choice did she have? "So, how are you doing? Are the girls enjoying college?"

"I guess. I hardly hear from Stephanie—I hope she isn't partying too much. Wren texts me about ten times a day. I worry she's lonely." Mattie's voice trembled.

"You must miss them. Is Wes around these days?"

Mattie didn't answer for several seconds, and when she did, she sounded like she was trying not to cry. "No. But I can't talk about him right now. It makes me—"

"Mattie…" It was awful being so far away, not able to give her sister a hug, or have a proper conversation.

"I'm okay. You just caught me at a bad time."

But when the call was over Sage couldn't help wondering if Mattie was having any good times these days.

SAGE SPENT THE rest of her weekend making chocolates. She

pulled out the molds for her Halloween treats—solid pumpkins in dark, milk and white chocolate. Also witches, ghosts and black cats.

Each mold was filled with her own special blended chocolate, then set aside to cool before packaging.

The work was repetitious and soothing.

She found herself thinking a lot about her mom. *Had* she regretted her marriage? If so, why hadn't she left? Was it because of them, her daughters? Or had she loved Hawksley, as well as Bill, and been torn between the two different men?

She would never find out the answers to these questions. Her mom was gone, and no one else could tell her.

But she did know her mother had loved them all enough to stay. She'd loved them enough to cook them meals and treats, to kiss their knees when they fell, and to tell them stories every night before tucking them in.

Maybe her father was right, and she'd been wrong to judge her mother so harshly.

Should that apply to Dawson, too?

AFTER THE ROUND-UP at the Circle C, Dawson did his best to focus on his new job and helping his daughter settle in with her new babysitters. Fortunately Savannah was a fast adapter. Nothing seemed to faze her. Soon all that was left was to move into their new house and they'd be completely settled.

True to his word, he made no effort to contact Sage. That didn't mean she wasn't in his thoughts, pretty much all day and all night. On Friday, when he took possession of his new house, Dawson took the day off work and kept Savannah home from the sitters. It didn't take long to transfer the possessions from their trailer to the new place.

His mother had been right about one thing. He needed more stuff.

And he didn't look forward to buying it. Maybe he should have accepted her help, after all, though at the time he'd been hoping Sage would be the one to help him furnish the new place.

He happened to be at the front door that afternoon when the mail carrier came by.

"Hey you must be the new owner," the man said, pulling a legal sized manila envelope out of his bag. "Welcome to the neighborhood. Here's your first official piece of mail."

The envelope had been forwarded from his legal firm in Reno.

Dawson thanked the guy, then sank onto the front stoop.

Savannah raced by him, carrying her backpack full of toys into her new bedroom. "Hey, Daddy. That's not helping."

"Just taking a break for a minute."

She carried on, and he closed his eyes, listening to her light footsteps tripping down the hall. The October sun was warm and healing on his face.

He let it soak in for a few minutes. Then he opened the package and scanned through the document. What he needed to see was on the last page. His signature… and hers.

She'd finally done it. Gina had signed the divorce papers.

He was free.

Trouble was—it didn't matter anymore.

MAYBE SHE'D TAKE her mountain bike out this weekend for a challenging ride, Sage thought, as she closed shop on Friday. Take advantage of the dry trails before the first big snow storm hit. It wouldn't be long. She'd seen frost on the grass during her ride to work this morning. Every day the trees were looking a little more naked, as they shed their summer foliage.

She cycled off Main Street, following her usual route. Someone had raked their leaves into a big pile on the road. She drove right through it, relishing the crunching of the dry leaves, the delicious fall scent—that was really about death—floating up in the air around her.

She thought about avoiding Bramble Lane. But that seemed cowardly.

Or maybe she just wanted a chance to see him. Even though it would hurt.

She passed the big mansions first. The home where her mother had been born. Great-Aunt Mabel was out on the porch, sipping tea, her shoulders covered in a green and brown afghan.

She pulled in for a moment to pass on the message from her father. Of course she worded it politely. Unfortunately there didn't seem to be any papers around the ranch that would help with the biography.

Eliza came out halfway through her explanation and Sage could tell her cousin didn't believe her.

The "Harrumph" she heard as she returned to her bike sounded a lot like her father's.

The houses in the next block were a little less grand, but still lovely. And now she was cycling past the third block and there was the "For Sale" sign—now covered over with a banner proclaiming: "Sold!"

How happy Tod must be with his latest commission.

Sage stopped pedaling allowing the bike to coast as Dawson's driveway came into view. His black truck was no longer dusty. He must have washed it.

And now she could see the house—hunkered in between two Mountain Ash, their red berries future fodder for the hardy winter birds. Sitting on the front steps was Savannah, the red door open behind her.

"Hi, Sage!"

When Savannah waved at her, and called her name a second time, Sage felt compelled to stop. She squeezed the brakes and planted her left foot on the ground. "Hi, Savannah. How do you like your new house?"

"It's big. And on Monday I have to start going to school." Her shoulders slumped. "Every day, except the weekend."

"School will be fun." Sage pulled her bike over the curb and set it to rest on the driveway, next to Dawson's truck.

"I don't know. Seems like a lot of responsibility."

She was something else, this girl of Dawson's. "Where's your daddy?"

"Taking a shower. When he's done, he's going to let me go play with a girl who lives down there." Savannah pointed to her left. Then she reached out for Sage's hand. "Want to come and see my house?"

"I shouldn't. Not unless your dad says it's okay."

"He will," Savannah gave her hand a tug. She was stronger than she looked.

Sage gave in, allowing the little girl to pull her over the threshold. She had to admit, she wasn't all that reluctant—she was curious to see if the inside was as nice as the exterior.

The layout of the interior was perfect, as were the colors, cool gray with white accents. Moldings on the doors and walls were generous and the floor was a simple, plank oak.

But—where was the furniture?

"Is the moving truck coming later?"

"No." Savannah's eyes were wide and innocent. "We're done. We put everything in the trailer into the house. See?"

She pointed out a couple of folding camp chairs against one wall in the living room. A tiny TV sat on the floor opposite. In the kitchen Sage recognized the dishes that Dawson had used in his trailer. There wasn't yet a table or chairs.

"So where's the trailer now, Savannah?"

"It's in a Sign-ment store, waiting to be sold."

"Consignment?"

Savannah nodded. "Want to see my room?"

The sound of running water, coming from the bathroom down the hall, suddenly stopped. "I have to leave, Savannah."

"Just *one look*. Pleease?"

She sounded so eager, Savannah couldn't resist. "Okay. But a really fast look."

At the door she saw a sleeping bag on the floor and several duffel bags open with clothes peeking out.

"My toys are here," Savannah said, pointing out some clear plastic tubs stacked in the opposite corner.

"Awesome. It's going to be pretty when you get some furniture moved in. But Savannah, I really have to go now. It was nice to see you and I hope you like your new school." She was backing into the hallway as she said this, but a sudden whiff of humidity, carrying the scent of a woodsy-smelling shampoo, told her she'd tarried just a little too long. Then she heard his voice, right behind her. "Like what I've done with the place?"

She turned in time to catch the guarded look in his eyes.

He wasn't dressed, but he had a towel around his waist at

least. Water glistened on his well-muscled chest, a few of the drops trickling down to the narrow plane of his stomach.

"It'll be easy to vacuum."

"That it will," His eyes held a question....but also, hope. "Did Savannah drag you in here? So far she's given tours to the lady who lives next door, two guys who get paid to maintain the gardens in the fancy houses up the street and a little girl out walking her dog."

"I'm being neighborly, right Daddy? That's how you make new friends."

"Well, I think it's okay to have an open house on moving day. But after that it's invitation only."

"Huh?"

Sage honestly didn't take in much of this exchange. She was remembering how Dawson had looked *without* a towel. And thinking it really wasn't appropriate to let her mind go there when a child was present.

"I'm going to put some clothes on. Sage, do you mind walking Savannah down the block to the house with the green door? The woman who lives there already popped over with a casserole."

Sage knew that woman. She'd been divorced for about two years. "A casserole, huh? I'll bet it's real tasty."

Dawson looked clueless. "I have no idea. We haven't eaten it, yet. Anyway, she has a five-year-old daughter, too, and I promised Savannah could go over. But just for an hour." He was looking at Savannah as he said this.

"Yes! Please take me, Sage!" Savannah took her hand and gave it an enthusiastic tug.

"Sure I will. It's no problem."

Sage all but dragged her out of the house and down the street. One quick rap on the green door, and Miranda Jenkins was revealed, her smile fading when she looked from Sage to Savannah, then back again. "Hello Sage. You know Dawson's daughter?"

"She's Daddy's friend," Sage announced, little realizing she was crushing hopes with that comment.

Seeing the disappointment on Miranda's face, Sage almost added that the situation wasn't how it appeared. But on second thought—why bother. She could let Dawson handle his own love life. Wasn't that what she'd asked him to do?

"Dawson will be back in an hour to pick her up," Sage said. Savannah and Miranda's daughter, Isabelle, had already run out the back door to the yard.

Mission accomplished, Sage headed down the street to retrieve her bike. But it wasn't there. Either it had been stolen or…

"I moved it to the back yard." Dawson was in faded jeans and a white T-shirt. His hair was partially dry already, but one strand had fallen over his forehead. He really did clean up well.

"Why'd you that?"

"Come here, Darlin'." He took her hand, pulled her in the front door and kissed her.

It wasn't as rough as the last one.

No, this kiss was thorough, and serious. The kind that said next step: bed.

She put a hand on his chest, but didn't have to push too hard to make him pause. "W-why did you do that?"

"Because it seems to me that you wouldn't be in this house right now unless you still cared."

Of course he was right. She could have waved at Savannah and just kept pedaling.

"According to our agreement, I was supposed to leave you alone. But I'm not a man who gives up easily. I was waiting for something Sage, and today it finally arrived. Let me show you…" He opened the front closet and pulled out a thick document, stapled in the left-hand top corner.

She only needed a glance. "Your divorce?"

"Yup. It's final."

The relief was all over his face, erasing lines, brightening his eyes and easing his smile so it seemed more loose and natural. Frankly, she felt pretty good, too. After all these years he was finally free.

He looped his arms around her waist and touched his head to hers. "There's a song where the guy sings that his woman made him a better man. It's really true for me. You have an inner light, Sage. It pulled me toward you from the start. The more I got to know you, the more I could see that there was another way for me to live my life. A better way."

Sage thought about his mother and how she'd claimed

Dawson was ready to change. That only showed how little Patricia really knew her son. "You never needed me to show you that. It was always in you. I love watching you with Savannah. You're a good father, Dawson. And a good man. Even Hawksley thinks so."

"You mean I already have my prospective father-in-law's good wishes?"

Her heart soared hearing those words. Not that she'd doubted Dawson's intentions. Not anymore. "Good wishes might be stretching things when it comes to Hawksley."

He pulled her in closer fitting their bodies snuggly and taking some of her weight in his arms. "I hit rock bottom the day you left me in Wyoming. But I made a promise to myself and I stuck with it. Five long years of saving and studying all came together the day I got the job offer from the Sheriff's Office."

"And I thought it was the rodeo that brought you to town."

"Wrong. It was you. The rodeo was icing on the cake—the grand finale to a career that served me well for a while."

"You really think you can quit cold turkey?"

"For you and Savannah? Absolutely. I hope you're okay with the house I bought. I picked it because it made me think of you."

His instincts were true. But why wouldn't they be. This man knew her better than anyone. Even better than her sisters and her best friends. "The house is perfect."

"I was so thankful when Tod let on that you'd inquired about it. Though by then I was already worried my plan was washed up. I never imagined it would take so long for you to accept my apology."

"It would have been easier if you hadn't waited five years to deliver it."

"Yeah. That was a bad call on my part. But I was determined that the next time I went near you it would be as a free man."

She had to admire that.

"But getting Gina to agree on divorce terms, and then sign the damn papers was a nightmare. For a marriage that only lasted a matter of months, we sure set a record when it came to ending it."

"I didn't make your job easy for you, either. I hung on to my anger too long. Wouldn't admit to myself that maybe you deserved a second chance." She'd been longing to touch him. Now she pressed her palm to his cheek, and he caught her hand and kissed it.

"So that stuff you said about the Sheriff?"

"Just a smokescreen. I'm sorry for that. Yes, we went out, but it's over and done for good. I never really loved him. How could I?"

"Darlin'—I feel like we have so much to talk about. But in fifty minutes I have to go pick up Savannah—And you have something I've been wanting for a very long time." He ran his hands down her waist to her hips, then to her butt.

His kiss was still imprinted on her lips. And she wanted more, too. "Better show me your new bedroom then."

"If you don't mind a mattress on the floor. It's all I've got."

"Not true, Dawson. You've also got me."

The End

The Carrigans of Circle C

Hawksley Carrigan, owner of the Circle C Ranch south of Marietta, Montana, always wanted a son to carry on the family name. Unfortunately for him, he ended up with four daughters

Book 1: Promise Me, Cowboy
Sage Carrigan's story

Book 2: Good Together
Mattie Carrigan's story

Book 3: Close to Her Heart
Dani Carrigan's story

Book 4: Snowbound in Montana
Eliza Bramble's story

Book 5: A Cowgirl's Christmas
Callan Carrigan's story

Available now at your favorite online retailer!

About The Author

USA Today Bestselling author C.J. Carmichael has written over 45 novels in her favorite genres of romance and mystery. She has been nominated twice for the *Romance Writers of America* RITA Award, as well as *RT Bookclub's* Career Achievement in Romantic Suspense award, and the *Bookseller's Best* honor.

She gave up the thrills of income tax forms and double entry book-keeping in 1998 when she sold her first book to Harlequin Superromance. Since then she has published over 35 novels with Harlequin and is currently working on a series of western romances with Tule Publishing. In addition C.J. Carmichael has published several cozy mystery series as an Indie author.

When not writing C.J. enjoys family time with her grown daughters and her husband. Family dinners are great. Even better are the times they spend hiking in the Rocky Mountains around their home in Calgary, and relaxing at their cottage on Flathead Lake, Montana.

Visit C.J.'s website at CJCarmichael.com.

Thank you for reading

Promise Me, Cowboy

If you enjoyed this book, you can find more from all our great authors at TulePublishing.com, or from your favorite online retailer.

Made in the USA
Columbia, SC
04 January 2019